WITHDRAWN

HONORS FOR APRIL HENRY

Edgar Award Finalist

Anthony Award Winner

ALA Best Books for Young Adults

ALA Quick Picks for Young Adults

Barnes & Noble Top Teen Pick

Maryland Black-Eyed Susan Book Award Winner

Missouri Truman Readers Award Winner

Texas Library Association Tayshas Selection

New York Charlotte Award Winner

Oregon Spirit Award Winner

Oregon Book Award Winner

One Book for Nebraska Teens

Nebraska Golden Sower Honor Book

South Dakota YA Reading Program Winner

THE
LONELY
DEAD

OTHER MYSTERIES BY APRIL HENRY

Girl, Stolen
The Night She Disappeared
The Girl Who Was Supposed to Die
The Girl I Used to Be
Count All Her Bones

THE POINT LAST SEEN SERIES
The Body in the Woods
Blood Will Tell

APRIL HENRY

THE LONELY DEAD

Christy Ottaviano Books

HENRY HOLT AND COMPANY

NEW YORK

Henry Holt and Company, *Publishers since 1866*
Henry Holt® is a registered trademark of Macmillan Publishing Group, LLC
175 Fifth Avenue, New York, New York 10010 • fiercereads.com

Library of Congress Cataloging-in-Publication Data
Names: Henry, April, author.
Title: The lonely dead / April Henry.
Description: First edition. | New York : Henry Holt and Company, 2019. |
Summary: When Adele, who possesses a paranormal
gift, is implicated in an investigation that involves the murder of her
ex–best friend Tori, she must work with Tori's ghost to find the killer.
Identifiers: LCCN 2018021064 | ISBN 9781250157577 (hardcover)
Subjects: | CYAC: Mystery and detective stories. | Supernatural—Fiction. |
Murder—Fiction. | Schizophrenia—Fiction. | Mental illness—Fiction.
Classification: LCC PZ7.H39356 Lo 2019 | DDC [Fic]—dc23
LC record available at https://lccn.loc.gov/2018021064

Our books may be purchased in bulk for promotional, educational, or
business use. Please contact your local bookseller or the Macmillan
Corporate and Premium Sales Department at (800) 221-7945 ext. 5442
or by e-mail at MacmillanSpecialMarkets@macmillan.com.

First edition, 2019 / Designed by April Ward
Printed in the United States of America

1   3   5   7   9   10   8   6   4   2

For Wendy Schmalz,
agent and friend over the course of twenty-five years
and literally dozens of books

NOT MAKING SENSE

Would anyone even hear me scream if something bad happened back in this wooded corner of Gabriel Park? Aside from the occasional dog walker, I rarely meet anyone on this path. A couple of months ago I did see a homeless guy crawl out of a dirty tent set up underneath a rhododendron, but I just walked faster and he didn't make eye contact.

It's a bleak fall day, close to sunset. Cutting through the park is the fastest route from the city bus stop to the apartment I share with my grandpa. In Portland, only elementary and middle school kids ride school buses. Once you're in high school, you have to take TriMet, the city transit system. Even if none of the stops are close to where you live.

After crossing the small wooden bridge over the stream, I pick up my pace as I enter the trees. My footfalls are muffled by the hard-beaten earth of the twisty path, spotted with puddles from yesterday's rain.

This section isn't like the rest of the park. No grass, no basketball courts, no paved paths, no playground equipment. Just towering evergreens, the way Portland must have looked two hundred years ago. The slanted late-afternoon light reveals a million shades of green and brown. Yellow-green ferns spring from the rust-colored needles blanketing the dark brown earth. The tree trunks are covered with velvety emerald moss, and the gray-green-needled branches of the trees slice the darkening sky.

It's hard to believe I'm in the middle of a city. This could be the fairy-tale forest where Little Red Riding Hood met the wolf, or Hansel and Gretel came across the witch's house. Back here, I've seen coyotes slink into the shadows, and once I even spotted a black-tailed deer bounding away into the trees.

As I round a corner, a girl calls out, "Adele?" Even though I can't quite place it, her voice is familiar. I stop. I don't see anyone, but I'm not nervous. I'm afraid of homeless guys, of drunk guys, of guys who might try to drag me into the bushes. Not of some girl who knows my name.

"Adele?" she calls again.

A flash of movement on my left. I squint in the gathering darkness. Through a gap in the branches, I see a girl sitting cross-legged under the green skirts of a tree, her back against the trunk. She lifts her hand and wiggles her fingers.

Tori Rasmussen. And for some reason, she's pretending she's not mad at me.

I start walking again. Whatever Tori wants to say, I don't want to hear it. Especially not after what happened—what I did—Saturday night. I don't want to be anywhere near her.

"No! Don't leave, Adele," she calls. "Please! Talk to me."

Against my better judgment, I turn back and push my way through the branches. One slaps me wetly in the face. I stop about ten feet from her. As usual, I feel hulking next to Tori, who's built like a sprite.

"What." I don't phrase it like a question.

"Adele?" Tori repeats. She looks both surprised and happy. Which doesn't make sense. The last time I saw her, she was screaming at me to get out of her sight.

"What are you doing here, anyway?" Tori lives a couple of miles from here, up in the West Hills in a house that's probably bigger than my whole apartment building. Why is she hanging out at the park? She wasn't even at school today. I know, because I looked, ready to duck out of sight. I couldn't avoid her friends, though. I saw the looks they shot me, the way they whispered behind their hands and rolled their eyes.

Tori isn't dressed like she's been out running or walking a dog. In fact, she isn't dressed for the weather at all. Now that I've stopped moving, I can feel the chilly November air even through my coat. Tori is wearing a peacock-blue halter dress that sets off her red hair and pale shoulders. Just looking at her bare legs and arms makes me shiver.

The thing is, I know that dress. It's the one Tori was wearing Saturday night. Which was nearly forty-eight hours ago. When I left her house, Tori and Luke were still fighting. Maybe they ended up in his car, driving around and arguing, and she eventually got out in a huff. And now she's hiding out to teach him some kind of lesson.

But for nearly two days? And how did she get here? Her bare feet are perfectly clean and white, her toes painted the same iridescent sheen as her dress.

She tilts her head to one side but doesn't answer my question. "You can hear me."

"Yeah," I say slowly. She's not making sense. "Are you okay, Tori? Aren't you cold?"

Her snub nose crinkles in confusion. "No. I'm not feeling much of anything."

So Tori's drunk. Or on drugs. My breath is hanging in a cloud. If it isn't freezing now, it will be as soon as the last light leaves.

"Even though I'm still furious with you, I'm just glad you're talking to me." She presses her lips together and shakes her head. "I've been calling and calling, and no one hears me."

Only then do I see it. A gray rope of mist falls from the back of her head like a braid. The other end disappears into the ground where she's sitting, a small rise of freshly turned earth surrounded by decades of reddish-brown pine needles.

On the nape of my neck, the hair rises. Next to Tori's thigh, a big toe is poking out from the dirt. The toe is grayish, and the nail is painted a familiar blue-green. The prickling spreads down my arms.

That rise is a grave.

And that grave? It's Tori's.

She's dead. But she doesn't know it.

JUST A LIE

No. I blink, rub my eyes, and look again. The grave is still there.

Only it can't be. That can't be a mound of fresh dirt. And Tori can't be sitting on top of it, talking to me.

Grandpa warned me this would happen. He said if I ever stopped taking my pills, I would go back to being delusional.

In my mind, I hear Dr. Duncan's soothing voice, the kind that invites confessions. The first time we talked, he said, "Adele, have you ever talked to a person no one else can see?" I was so young that I didn't realize it was a terrible idea to say yes.

Seeing things that aren't really there, hearing voices say awful things—the doctors and my grandpa all agree these are signs of my mental illness. I'm schizophrenic, just like my mom and grandma were. Both me and my mom were prescribed antipsychotics. Unlike her, though, I've been taking my meds. At least until two weeks ago, when I accidentally missed a pill. The next morning, I woke up feeling so *alive*. And then I decided to keep skipping them and see what happened.

The answer is Tori. Tori happened. And the reality is that she's not dead and I'm not talking to her ghost or spirit or whatever. She's just a lie that my broken brain is telling me. Just because she wasn't at school today doesn't mean she's dead. My mind's trying to make me feel bad, conjuring up a dead Tori to punish me for what I did Saturday.

The talking Tori, the grave I think contains a dead Tori—none of it's real. I make myself turn away from the hallucination. Make myself stop talking. Tell myself to stop listening. By acting as if all this is real, I'm giving it power.

"Adele?" Tori says anxiously. "Where are you going?"

Pain pricks behind my right eye. I have to get home before someone sees me talking to no one. If Grandpa ever finds out . . .

With one hand raised to shield my face from branches, I start to push my way back out.

"Wait!" Her voice turns frantic. "Adele! Please help me. Something's wrong. I keep trying to leave, but for some reason I can't."

"Shut up. Please. Just shut up." I pause but don't turn around. "You're just in my mind. You're not real."

I'm breaking Dr. Duncan's rules, the ones I kept until the medication made the hallucinations go away. Don't interact with them. The more you do, the more you'll fall into the abyss of your own insanity. Remove yourself from the place where you imagine you see the dead. If you can't, ignore them.

"What do you mean I'm not real?" Tori forces a laugh. "I'm right here. Adele. Please." Her voice breaks. "Please, please, please. I know I haven't been that nice to you lately, but—"

Forgetting the rules, I whirl around and cut her off. "What do you mean you haven't been that nice to me *lately*? You haven't been nice to me for years!"

Our friendship began the first day of kindergarten, when we were seated next to each other. When you're little, you can become best friends just because you both like Oreos and SpongeBob.

Back then, it didn't matter that my clothes came from thrift stores and hers from Nordstrom. It didn't matter that with my dad in college, my mom paid for groceries with food stamps while her mom had a housekeeper who did the shopping. For her sixth birthday, I gave her a SpongeBob squirt gun I had gotten from a cereal box, and she said she liked it more than all the expensive toys she received.

But as we got older, we began to pull apart. First there were my secrets, which I learned never to share. And as Tori got older, she got busier. Her parents enrolled her in a million after-school activities, like gymnastics and horseback riding. Things there was no sense in even asking my parents about.

At least back then I still had parents.

Then in second grade, my dad got what he thought was the flu but was really meningitis. That morning he'd been laughing as he gave me a piggyback ride to the bus stop. That night, feverish and nauseated, he went to bed early in the guest room, complaining about a pounding head and stiff neck. When my mom tried to wake him the next morning, she found him cold. I woke to her screams. She was never the same. Two years later, she was killed in a car accident and I had to move in with my grandpa. When he discovered I thought I could talk to dead people, he hustled me off to a psychiatrist. The pills Dr. Duncan prescribed took away my hallucinations but left me slow and anxious, unable to concentrate. Not exactly top-shelf friend material.

When we started middle school, Tori made new friends. She became one of the popular people, and I became the kind of girl no one much notices. Now it's like we were never close.

"You have to admit that you were always a little weird, and you've only gotten weirder." Tori quirks one auburn eyebrow. "Remember how you tried to convince me there was an invisible bird in my basement? You'd even hold out your finger and claim it was landing on it." She rolls her blue eyes. Here in the shadows, I shouldn't be able to see her so clearly. My imagination must be coloring in this hallucination more vibrantly than real life.

Just like it did the parakeet in her basement. It had a sky-blue chest and back, with a white-and-black-striped head and wings. It could flutter four or five feet in any direction, but the thin tether of mist that ran from the back of its head to the concrete floor prevented it from going too far. A few weeks ago in Western Art, we saw a photo of *The Goldfinch*, a famous painting of a bird chained by its foot to a bird feeder. I gasped. Tori looked over, and I knew she remembered too.

Back then, when I told my mom about the parakeet, she said it must have been buried under the concrete basement floor. And she warned me to stop talking about it, even to Tori. But later Dr. Duncan told me that all the dead and buried things I've seen acting like they're alive—dogs and cats, parakeets, and occasionally people—are all in my head.

But sometimes I wonder. If I had somehow dug down through the basement's concrete floor, would I have discovered a handful of tiny bones? So light you could hold them in your palm and not even tell they were there?

Seeing that painting in art class must be why I'm imagining Tori talking about the bird now.

"Okay," she says. "You think you're imagining me."

I nod. "I *know* that."

"You think you're mentally ill."

"I stopped taking my meds." I rub the spot on my temple that feels like it's being impaled.

"What meds?"

I don't answer her. Tori should know what I'm talking about, since she's really me, or at least a splinter of me. I don't like the way the drugs bleed the color from everything. How they make me feel dizzy and drowsy and sick to my stomach. I'm seventeen years old. Don't I get to feel alive?

"And for some reason, now you think I'm dead," she continues. "Which is really crazy."

Great. Even my hallucinations are calling me insane.

"You're not real." I close my eyes, put my hands over my ears. But I can still hear her.

"Of course I'm real, Adele. And I'm definitely not dead."

The thing is, even though I know the Tori I'm talking to isn't real, what about the grave she's perched on?

I open my eyes and drop my hands from my ears. For a moment, I decide to act like it's all real, the living girl and the dead one. It's the logic you use in dreams. Like when you suddenly find yourself flying with just your arms, or you can swim underwater without needing to breathe. You just go with it and see where it takes you.

Maybe I could even be dreaming now. The thought fills me with relief.

"Look down," I tell Tori. "I'm pretty sure that's your own self you're sitting on. Check that out." I point at the object sticking up out of the dirt. "What's that?"

"It's a toe," she says slowly, looking back and forth from her own toes to the one emerging from the ground. The nail polish is the same shade.

"Right. *Your* toe. Just like up here someplace is your head." I move to the other end of the mound and begin to scoop and scrape where the tether of mist disappears. Tori gets to her feet and watches, her hand over her mouth. The jumble of needles and earth is fresh. Someone has tried to tamp it down, but it's still loose, easy to move. In only a few seconds, we both see it: the face of the dead Tori.

Her flesh is waxy and pale. Her eyes aren't completely closed. A rim of bloodshot white shows at the bottom. Dirt rests between her lips, like that time I got her to take a bite of a mud pie by double-dog daring her.

Tori looks down at her dead self and begins to scream.

TWELVE YEARS EARLIER

IF THE DEAD ARE ALWAYS ALIVE

was five when I first learned I could see the dead. Even smell and touch and talk to them.

My mom had brought me to her friend Pam's house. She and Pam settled around the kitchen table with cups of coffee and shooed me out to play in the bright June sunshine. Not that there was anything or anyone to play with in the fenced backyard.

I was drawing in the dirt with a stick—I was just learning how to spell my name—when I spotted the black dog. He was asleep between two rosebushes in the far corner of the yard, his nose resting on his paws.

When I walked up to him, he raised his head. His muzzle was white, as was the fur around his rheumy eyes. But when he saw me looking at him, his tail started to thump.

"Good dog." I held out my free hand, making a fist

the way my mom had taught me. He sniffed, then licked the top of my hand with his warm pink tongue. When I scratched behind his ears, he sighed in pleasure.

He smelled like wet fur and stale dog food, but I didn't mind. Because this was a dog, and he wanted to be my friend! Our apartment didn't allow pets. But just for this moment, I could pretend he belonged to me.

I raised the stick in my hand. He whined, low in his chest, then slowly pushed himself to his feet.

Turning, I threw it as far as I could. Which was only about six feet. But the dog didn't move.

I pointed. "Go get it, boy!"

Even though he whimpered, he stayed where he was.

Maybe he needed more of a challenge. I walked over to the stick, picked it up, and shook it. He let out a little woof. I threw it again. It was now about fifteen feet from him.

This time, the dog gathered himself and started to move toward it. But before he reached it, he stopped with a jerk. A silver-gray rope ran from the base of his skull to the ground, tethering him. It looked filmy, like it was made of fog. He pulled, but it didn't give. With a tired huff, he slowly moved back to his original spot and lay down.

Behind me, my mom called my name through the screen door.

I didn't move. "Can't we stay a little longer?"

"Honey, we don't have time. Sorry."

I squeezed the dog around the neck. His fur was

rough against my cheek. I whispered goodbye before I ran inside.

"They have a doggy, Momma." I hopped up and down in the kitchen with excitement. "He let me pet him, but he's tied up, so he can't play fetch with me."

Pam's eyes went wide. "We used to have a dog. But he died two years ago."

"He's not dead." I pointed out the window. The dog raised his head from his paws. "He's right there." He let out a yip. "Can't you hear him?"

"That's where we buried Oliver." Pam's gaze went from me to the window. She took one step back and then another. Her hands came up as if to keep me away. "How does she know that?"

My mom looked past me. Something about how her eyes narrowed told me she saw Oliver, too. She grabbed my upper arm, hard enough it hurt. Her laugh sounded like broken glass. "Oh, Adele's got such an active imagination. You know, only children."

I stamped my foot and pointed. "But he's right there."

Mom was already dragging me toward the front door. "Adele must have guessed. The earth is probably still disturbed back there."

Once we were outside, she didn't even buckle me in my booster seat. She just shoved me in the car, slammed the door, threw herself in the front seat, and started driving. Fast. I could hear her muttering to herself, but I couldn't make out any words.

After a few blocks, my mom pulled over, turned off

the car, and got in the back seat with me. She cupped my face with her cold hands.

"Listen to me, Adele. This is serious." Her brown eyes, the same color as mine, drilled into me. "I've been hoping I was wrong, but you and I, we have a big secret."

"What secret?" I liked secrets. Secrets meant things like presents and being allowed to lick the cake bowl even though it was almost dinnertime.

"We can see the dead."

"What?"

She took her hands away and pressed one to her mouth. "That dog in Pam's backyard? You might think he's alive, but he's not. He's dead."

My face got hot. Even at five, I knew what *dead* meant. Dead meant you couldn't move or play anymore. That it was all over.

But that clearly wasn't true for Oliver.

"Oliver wasn't dead. He was just old. He licked me."

"No, Adele." Mom shook her head. "The truth is that dog is nothing but buried bones. Even if you and I can still see him."

"So he's a ghost?" She wasn't making sense. And she was starting to scare me.

"I don't know." She shook her head, her eyes un-focused. "I don't know if we make the dead come alive for a little bit or if they're always alive in some way, but only certain people can see them." Her eyes pierced me again. "Listen to me. You can never tell anyone you see the dead. It disturbs people. If you think an animal or a person might really be dead, look for that tether from the back of their head. Or if they look fuzzy or see-through, that's another sign. The longer they've been dead, the fainter they get. The dead are lonely, so terribly lonely. It takes a lot of strength, but you have to ignore them, no matter how much it makes your head hurt. Especially don't talk to them if other people can see you. They'll call you crazy."

"I'm not crazy!" I was a little uncertain as to what *crazy* actually was, except for wrong. I had heard my grandpa call my mom that before she stormed out of his apartment, dragging me by one arm. But maybe he was right. Because what my mom was saying didn't make any sense.

She put her hands on my shoulders and gave me a little shake. "Imagine if Pam had seen you. She's not like you and me—she couldn't see that dog. All she would have seen was you." She shook me again, making her silver locket bounce on her chest. "To her, it would look like you were talking to nothing and patting the empty air."

My lower lip jutted out. "Oliver's not nothing. He's not dead. He was right there! You're lying! He's alive!" I could still feel his fur against my face, hear the sound of his labored breathing.

She shook me harder. "Adele! You have to listen! People like us have been killed because other people were afraid of what we can do. When we can't really *do* anything! We can't make others see what we do. We can't bring the dead back to life. All we can do is talk to them if we're near their bones."

"And pet them," I said stubbornly, still not wanting to believe her.

She took a ragged breath. "Do you know what a witch is?"

"They have pointed noses, and their skin is green." I thought some more. "And they fly on brooms. And they're bad."

"Well, we're none of those things, but if you tell people you can see the dead, some of them are going to think you're a witch." She gave me another shake. "Or mentally ill. Or a liar."

"You're scaring me, Momma."

She lifted her hands away from my shoulders. I saw they were trembling.

"Good. I'm glad you're scared. This is serious. You have to keep it a secret. And never even hint about it to your dad—and especially Grandpa. Seeing the dead is the reason your grandma's gone."

EVERY TIME
I TRY TO LEAVE

"Stop screaming," I tell Tori now. "It's hurting my ears." It's also not helping the pain in my head.

The shrieks stop, but not the protests. "I'm not dead!" Tori says. "I'm not!" She keeps her gaze fastened on my face, not looking any lower. I'm still on my knees at the head of the makeshift grave.

At this point, I'm not too certain myself what's true. The Tori who's screaming and arguing—she's probably not real. But what about the dead Tori whose face I just uncovered? Is that Tori real?

"This is you, Tori," I say to myself as much as to her. "Your body, anyway."

"No it's not. *I'm* me." She pokes herself in the chest. "That's just a thing." She flicks her hand dismissively. "A mannequin, something made up to look like me. It's a sick joke. You know, for a TV show or something." She squints up at the trees as if searching for hidden cameras.

Tori needs to calm down, but she won't if she can still see her dead self. I push the dirt back into place. Under my fingers, the dead girl's face is cold and hard, as inanimate as a metal table. When I graze the tether at the back of her head, it feels like cool, plush fabric.

"I can't be dead. I can't," the other Tori says as I get to my feet. "This is all a dream. I must be asleep." She extends her bare arm. "Pinch me."

I pinch her upper arm. Hard. Not just to convince her, but to convince myself. Was my mom right, and Grandpa and Dr. Duncan wrong? I pinch Tori's skin until she yelps.

"See?" I lift my hand from her unblemished arm. "It doesn't wake you up, and it doesn't leave a mark. I might be able to see you and talk to you and even touch you, but I can't really change what you are now. What you were the second you died."

Tori grabs my wrist. Her fingernails dig in painfully, but when she lets go, there's no sign. Just like when that old dog Oliver slobbered on me but left no trace of wetness behind.

When Tori sees my unmarked wrist, she collapses into my arms. I hold her while she cries. She's warm and pliable, unlike the girl in the grave. This close, I see the dark red line that runs across her throat. She wasn't choked with hands, but with something like a thin rope. Other, shallower red marks run from just under her chin to the hollow of her throat. Tori must have clawed her own skin, trying to save herself.

On the back of her neck, the dark line ends in two purple-red oval bruises. I place my thumb on top of one. It's about the same size. My stomach drops as the pain in my head worsens. Even though parts of Saturday night are blurry, surely I would remember if I'd killed Tori. It's just that I have big hands, I tell myself. I'm a big girl, as Tori has pointed out more than once.

Finally she lifts her head. Even though I heard her crying, her face isn't red and blotchy. "If I'm dead, how can you hear me? I tried talking to other people. But no one answered."

"My mom told me it runs in my family. My grandpa and my doctor just say we're schizophrenic." I press on my temple, trying to counteract the pain, but it doesn't help.

She grimaces. "What do other people like me say?"

"I've only actually talked to one other dead person. I can only see the dead where their bones are. Mostly I just see pets buried in the yard by their owners. Like that parakeet in your basement."

Her snub nose wrinkles. "Does this mean I'm in limbo?"

"I think the Catholics did away with that."

"Well, I'm clearly not in heaven." She looks around. "So is this hell? Being stuck here with no one to talk to besides you?"

"Thanks a lot, Tori."

She rolls those baby blues. "You know what I mean. And every time I try to leave, this won't let me." She reaches up and grabs the rope of mist fastened to the back of her head. It's silvery, with milky edges, about a dozen feet long. Tori pulls it so hard her biceps pop up, but the corpse in the ground doesn't move even a millimeter.

"That looks like the dress you were wearing Saturday," I say. "So was that when you died?"

"I don't know. I don't remember much about Saturday night. We were doing shots, and after that it's more like a few mental pictures here and there."

"What's the last thing you remember?" I brace myself.

"Being at the party. Yelling at you. And at Luke. We broke up."

"You did?" I can't name the emotions roiling in me. I have a sudden flash of Luke's green eyes and then remind myself that probably none of this is true. Tori's not dead, and she and Luke Wheaten are still together.

Still, what if it *is* real? "There's marks on your neck." I touch my own throat. "I think someone strangled you. So who was it?"

"I have no idea. All I know is when I woke up I was under this stupid tree. And now according to you, I'll never be able to make up with Luke. I'll never talk to my friends again." Her voice breaks. "I want to see my parents."

It's full dark now. I have to get back before my grandpa does and get myself calmed down. Act like I'm my old zombie self. If he finds out I haven't been taking my pills . . .

"Tori, I'm so late. I have to go."

"Don't leave me here alone." While a command is much more Tori's style, this is a plea.

"I can't stay. I'm already late."

Her jaw sets. "Then you have to tell the police I'm here."

"I can't do that! First of all, there's a pretty good chance you're not. I don't want to end up in a mental hospital."

"Please, Adele, I'm the one who's going crazy here. If you won't do it for me, then do it for my family. If I'm really dead, they deserve to know where I am."

"The caller ID will show that I'm the one who called."

"Isn't there a 7-Eleven down the street? With one of those old pay phones in front? Just call 9-1-1. Tell them you were in the park and you saw a dog pawing at what looked like a grave. And then hang up. By the time they check it out, you'll be long gone."

"Okay." The word isn't all the way out of my mouth before she envelops me in a hug. Every bad thing that's come between us over the years fades a bit under the force of that hug.

I finally pull back. This is the last time we'll talk. Once I'm back on my meds, this Tori will disappear.

And even if she's not a hallucination, once her corpse is taken away, this version of her will have to go wherever her body does.

Before I leave, I brush the dirt off the dead girl's face again, telling Tori that it will make it easier for the police to find the body. After giving her one final hug, I push my way out of the branches. Only a combination of muscle memory and luck keeps me on the dark path.

Finally I reach the road. When there's a break in the cars, I run across, my pack thumping against my back. In my chest, my heart thumps even faster.

I want nothing more than to be back in my apartment. I'll take a pill tonight and another tomorrow morning, and I'll keep taking them until everything is hazy. Until I forget this ever happened.

DOESN'T DESERVE TO

As I cut across the street, I wonder if putting my turtleneck over my mouth will actually change my voice. Even though people in movies are always doing that kind of thing, does it really work? I decide to pitch my voice lower and rougher. It's already pretty low. Maybe they'll even think I'm a guy.

The 7-Eleven is part of a small strip mall with a windowless bar on one end and a martial arts place on the other. I peer inside through taped up ads for cigarettes and beer. The clerk is facing away from me, reading a magazine. It's the lady who's nearly as old as grandpa. She's sold me Doritos, Lay's chips, and Fritos of all flavors, as well as the occasional handheld fruit pie.

The scratched and dented pay phone is mounted outside. A call costs fifty cents, but when I check my wallet, I don't have any coins. Maybe I should just take off. But I remember Tori weeping on my shoulder. Despite everything she's done, everything she's said, if what just happened was real, she doesn't deserve to spend another night out in the open.

My eyes settle on the words printed on the phone. It's free to make an emergency call.

When I pick up the black receiver, it's heavy in my sweaty hand. The shiny metal cord reminds me of the silvery rope of mist running from the back of Tori's head. That tether, Tori, the dead version of her: Any or all of these might or might not be real.

I press *9*, *1*, and then *1* again.

"Police, fire, or medical?"

"Police." I'm trying so hard to make my voice deep it cracks.

"What is the nature of your emergency?"

"I was just in Gabriel Park, and I found a grave."

"A grave?" Does the dispatcher's voice betray surprise?

I realize I'm going to have to be more specific. "In that wooded part. Past the dog park. She's underneath the biggest tree."

Wait—wasn't I supposed to say something about a dog digging up a grave?

"She?" the dispatcher echoes. "Who's *she*?"

Cursing myself for being an idiot, I hang up.

THIS GAME

Waiting for the light to turn, I check the time on my phone. My grandpa is due home any moment. I don't want him asking questions about where I've been. He's told me more than once that dealing with my grandma's and mom's mental illness almost killed him. And even though I know he loves me, he's also made it clear he couldn't—wouldn't—go through it again.

What will happen if he figures out I've stopped taking my pills? Will he kick me out? Put me in a mental hospital? Either way, my life would be even worse than it is when I'm on the pills.

I hear the cop car before I see it. Red and blue lights flashing, speeding down the street toward me. Cars pull over to let it pass. The WALK sign blinks on, but I have to stay put.

And then the police car turns. Toward the park.

Toward where Tori, in some form or another, might be waiting.

I imagine the cop getting out of the car, flashlight at the ready. Will he—or she—be able to find the biggest tree? And what will be under it? A grave? Or nothing at all?

Shivers chase their way down my spine. The orange DON'T WALK sign is back on. After the lights cycle through again, I'm going to have to run to have any hope of making it home before Grandpa. Run toward my old medicated life, the one I don't want back.

The last two weeks I've felt more alive than I have in the last nearly seven years. In class, I no longer feel the insistent pull of sleep. Teachers keep looking surprised when I raise my hand. I've even lost nine pounds without trying.

If I start taking the pills again, it won't be long until I'm back to being the old Adele. Anxious Adele, who has trouble concentrating. Adele with her gummy mouth and shuffling walk. The pills make me feel like I'm seventy-seven, not seventeen.

On the other hand, if I hadn't started flushing my pills, I wouldn't have done that stupid thing at the party Saturday night.

And today I paid the price. I've slipped back into seeing things that aren't there.

Haven't I?

The light finally changes, and I run across the street. I dart through the parking lot, which doesn't have assigned spaces, scanning for Grandpa's truck, then start down the walk. I'm so busy checking that I run straight into Charlie Lauderdale.

Or rather, into the laundry basket he's carrying. He loses his grip on one side. It droops, scattering dirty clothes all over the even dirtier walkway.

"Charlie?" I have no idea where Charlie lives, but it's definitely not in my complex. No one else my age lives here. The twelve apartments are mostly occupied by older people or single moms with little kids. Having him appear on my apartment walkway is so weird I wonder if I'm hallucinating again.

"Hey, Adele." Charlie's tall and thin, verging on skinny. The tall part is new, and he doesn't seem comfortable with it. In high school, we've had a few classes together, but that's about it. He went to a different middle school. All I know about him is he's smart and quiet. Maybe even quieter than me. He's the kind of guy who's on the robotics team.

Even though the only light is at the top of the staircase, I can see a flush creeping up his neck. Awkwardly shifting the basket to one hip, he leans down and starts picking up the spilled laundry. I help. His face gets even redder as I add a sock and a sweater to the basket.

"You live here?" I ask. Although why else would he be here with a basket of laundry?

"As of last weekend." The redness has reached his face.

"Welcome to the 'hood." Leaning over, I snag the last item, which reveals itself to be a contraption of white elastic straps, and OMG, is that some kind of pouch? I realize it's a jockstrap.

I am holding Charlie Lauderdale's jockstrap.

I fling it into the laundry basket and wipe my hand on my pants as Charlie closes his eyes, his face scarlet.

"Sorry!" As soon as I say it, I wish I hadn't said anything. Better for both of us to pretend this moment never happened. "Um, I guess I'd better go." I start to push past him.

Above his shoulder, I see something that makes me freeze. The light is on in our apartment. And a shadow is moving over the curtain, toward the front door.

When my grandpa opens it, he's going to be wondering why I'm late. What if he figures out I'm off my meds before I have a chance to start taking them again?

I need to stop that thought before it starts. I need to give him something else to worry about.

The door creaks open. Turning, I put my palms on either side of Charlie's face, my fingertips just under his jaw. I ignore his sucked-in breath. My improvised plan is to cover his mouth with my thumbs and then kiss them. It's a game kids used to play on the playground when we were in fourth grade. Making out passionately with our thumbs while our onlooking classmates gagged dramatically.

But Charlie doesn't know this game. His shoulders stiffen as I move in to press my lips on my own thumbs. He suddenly lifts his head so my thumbs are no longer stacked on his lips but just underneath.

And instead of kissing my thumbs, I press my lips against Charlie's warm, soft ones. He smells like peppermint.

Something light drops on my foot. His basket is spilling again.

"Adele!" Grandpa sounds shocked.

"Coming!" I yell. Then I push past Charlie and run up the stairs.

STILL SHARP ENOUGH
TO SLASH

race up the staircase. Behind me, Charlie makes a soft noise. Of protest? Confusion? Regret?

My mind is whirling. Talking to a hallucination, kissing a boy—what's *wrong* with me? If I hadn't stopped taking my pills, none of this would have happened.

And what about tomorrow, when I see Charlie in health class? What exactly am I going to say? *I had to kiss you to cover up how I'd just been talking to a dead girl.*

"Hi!" I hurry past Grandpa and into our overheated apartment, making my voice bright and avoiding eye contact. "Sorry I'm late getting dinner started. I was doing homework."

As I drop my backpack on the floor next to our old flowered couch, I sneak a peek at Grandpa. His face is nearly as red as Charlie's was.

"This boy, Adele." He swallows. "How long have you been—seeing him?"

"He's just a friend." I hang my coat on a hook, then walk into the kitchen and grab a pot from the cupboard. The soles of my feet are slick in my shoes. In the bright light of the kitchen, what I thought happened in the park seems ridiculous. How could I have imagined I was talking to Tori? How could I have actually believed she was dead?

I just need to swallow a pill tonight. And then tomorrow I'll wake up without any hallucinations. Without any delusions.

These past two weeks were a test to see if I could be normal, but I failed. My grandpa and the doctors are right. I'm mentally ill.

Now I need my grandpa to chalk up any weirdness to Charlie. "We were just doing our homework together in the laundry room." I turn on the water and let it run until it's hot, then fill the pot and put it on the stove.

"Do you kiss all your friends?" Grandpa's silvery-gray eyes meet mine for a second. "I don't want you alone with him." Looking away, he rubs his twisted hands together. The arthritis means he can't work as a mechanic anymore. And even though all his friends are retired, he can't afford to. So he's stuck behind the counter at AutoZone. Because of me. Not that he ever says that. He's not much on saying *I love you*, but he shows it in how he acts.

"We're just friends," I repeat as I grab a knife and cutting board. "That's all." Even that part's not true. Until tonight, I haven't said much more than hi to Charlie. He and I are on the same level at high school, the kind of people who can walk down the hall without attracting attention. We're both so good at being nearly invisible that we've barely noticed each other. And even if we did, I bet he wouldn't be interested. I'm a little bit shorter, but I'm sure I outweigh him.

With a thwack, I chop off the root end of an onion. I repeat the move on the other side, then peel off the translucent yellow skin.

As I start to dice the onion, Grandpa lets out a huff and shakes his head. "I trust you, Adele, but you still can't have a boy over when I'm not here." He covers the pot of water so it will boil faster.

What he probably thinks but doesn't say is *I never thought a boy would be interested in you*. Grandpa is good at not saying things. Like: *Never talk about your mom and grandma—my daughter and wife—because it hurts too much*. Or: *Never mention how you used to see things, the same way they did*.

I've been on medication for nearly seven years. Now that I've tasted what life is like when I'm really alive, it's going to hurt so much to go back. Angry tears spring to my eyes. The sharpness of the chopped onion gives me an excuse for my wet eyes, just like Charlie gives me an excuse for my flushed cheeks and the damp half-moons under my arms.

"Okay. I'll never have him over." I sigh like it's a disappointment, then tip the onions into a frying pan and add a little bit of olive oil. "Could you rinse some lettuce for salad?" It's one of the few cooking tasks Grandpa can still do. His fine motor skills are shot, especially at the end of the day. But he never complains. Just like he never complains about having to be a parent again when he's nearly seventy.

"Charlie was a big help with my homework. I just gave him a peck. There's nothing more to it than that." I mince garlic while remembering the softness of his lips under mine. He and his family must have moved into Unit D. Mrs. Jimenez lived there forever, at least until her son put her in a nursing home last month.

Grandpa twists his lips in a worried way as he tears the lettuce into a bowl.

I add the garlic to the pan, then hamburger that I break up with a wooden spoon. I rummage around in the fridge. A red pepper still looks pretty good, so it gets diced and added, followed by a couple of zucchini. I add a shake of dried oregano and two of basil.

"That smells real good, Adele," Grandpa says as he puts the lettuce in a bowl. "You're turning into a regular chef." His praise, meant as a peace offering, just makes me want to cry even more. As soon as I'm back on my meds, the nausea and heartburn that normally plague me will come back. And I won't care about much of anything anymore.

When I lift the lid, the pot of water is boiling. I shake in some salt, then pour in pasta. Grandpa finishes the salad while I add some jarred sauce to the vegetables and meat, then drain the pasta and mix it in.

We eat mostly in silence. As he gets up to put his plate

in the dishwasher, Grandpa says, "You just need to be careful, Adele. You don't need to be stirring things up."

What he means is that if I die without ever getting married and having kids, then our family's curse dies with me. Whether it's mental illness or the kind of gift no one would want, either way it will be gone.

"Okay. Right." I don't bother to hide my sadness. He'll think it's about being kept from Charlie, when really it's about going back to being the half-alive Adele I was two weeks ago.

Before I start back on the pills, there's one last thing I want to check. "I'm going to take out the garbage." I pull out the white plastic liner before he can see it's only half full.

The garbage and recycling bins are in the back of the building, lined up on a concrete pad. It's also the place where the orange-and-white tabby kitten lives. Or at least its spirit does. It used to watch me from the bushes, so it was a while before I saw the tether and realized it was dead.

"Kitty?" I call. "Kitty?" My eyes scan the hedge where it used to hide. No answer. Finally I open the dumpster's black rubber lid and toss in the bag.

Behind me, I hear a meow. I turn. It's the same half-grown cat I used to see, even though almost seven years have passed.

I scratch the cat's head, run my hand down its body. Under my palm, its back vibrates as it starts to purr. My grandpa acts like only bad things come of seeing the dead, but this one is good. Or at the very least, neutral.

Before I leave, I give the kitten one last scratch behind the ears.

Back in the apartment, I lock the door to the bathroom, then open the medicine cabinet. In the metal back is the slit my grandpa says was for used razor blades. Lost somewhere in between the walls must be a pile of rusty metal, still sharp enough to slash.

The orange pill bottle is light in my hand. Funny how something that weighs so little can make the difference between sane and insane, between alive and something that's only a semblance.

But not taking the pills was like playing with fire. And I got burned.

After I close the cabinet, I stare into my own dark eyes, set off by my pale skin. I look like my mom. Only she was as thin as a knife's edge. Even her eyes could cut you.

I twist off the cap and shake a pill into my hand. In the distance, I hear a siren. And then another. And another.

I put the toilet lid down, then stand on top and push aside the dusty cream-colored curtain. In the park, the flashing red and blue lights of at least a dozen police cars light up the air.

For there to be that many cops, they must have found something. Something real.

They must have found a body.

Her body.

Instead of swallowing the pill, I step down off the toilet, lift the lid, and toss in the pill.

And then I flush.

BURY ME DEEP

tried crossing my legs, but it didn't help. I had to pee. My problem was that the bathrooms weren't even in this section of the End of the Oregon Trail Interpretive Center.

If I asked to go, Mrs. Whipple would just tell me to wait until our visit was over. Even with a couple of parent volunteers, her head was on a swivel trying to keep track of our class. Several fourth-grade school groups were visiting the museum. Some kids were in the dress-up area, trying on cowboy hats and petticoats. Others were dipping strings into melted wax to make candles or arguing about what to pack in the replica wagon bed.

"Aren't you hot?" Tori asked the sweaty-looking guy playing the storekeeper in charge of various boxes and bags labeled FLOUR, BACON, and COFFEE. It was a warm day in late May. We were all in shorts, but the museum reenactors were stuck wearing layers and long sleeves as if it were really 1850.

"I am quite comfortable, young scribe," the man said. Tori had a notebook—we all did—because later we had to write a report about life on the trail. Mrs. Whipple had already told us the Oregon Trail was actually the world's longest graveyard. Ten percent of the people who set out died before making it to their new homes.

I crossed my legs in the other direction, but it didn't work. I couldn't wait any longer. Luckily, the other students provided plenty of cover. I slipped behind them and then out the door.

The restrooms were housed in a separate building. I pushed open the door to the ladies' room and headed straight back toward one of the three empty stalls. When I came out, I noticed what I hadn't been able to see from the entrance: a girl tucked in the corner, under the paper towel dispenser. Her knees were drawn up to her chest. A blue bonnet with a long bill hid her face, but she looked about my age. Her brown hair fell in two tight braids nearly to her waist. On top of her long gray dress was an apron that might have once been white.

"Are you okay?" I asked. Was she sick? Or maybe she was just tired of having to playact in front of dozens of kids.

"You can see me?" Her voice sounded rusty. Tired.

"Of course."

"I am shy of trusting you." The bill of her bonnet waggled back and forth as she shook her head. "You are not real, I warrant it."

Her pretending to be confused by me made more sense than the other reenactors' casual acceptance of a crowd of strange children wearing cartoon T-shirts, carrying cell phones, and peppering them with questions.

"Do they teach you how to talk all old-timey like that?"

She sighed. "You take pains to discommode me. Do not be such a wiseacre."

I was more and more impressed. "Wow, the other actors don't talk nearly as good as you. I can't even understand half of what you're saying."

"Are you here only to vex me?"

Her annoyed tone let me decipher her words. She was pretending like I was the one who wasn't making sense. I decided to ignore that part of her act.

"My name's Adele. What's yours?"

"Rebecca. After all these years, what has made *you* sensible of *me*?"

She must be asking why I was here. "My whole class is here. It's part of the Oregon Trail unit. So do you tell everyone what it was like for kids on the trail?"

"Sometimes we drove the teams or fetched water or gathered buffalo chips. But for the most part, we children did as everyone else. Walked. Walked and walked and walked." She heaved a sigh. "Such a getting to Oregon. And of course, we were not spared perishing."

"Perishing? You mean dying?"

She nodded. "Even the smallest. After Mrs. Kohler died giving birth, her babe passed just two days later. Mr. Turner's son was only three when the fever took him.

My cousin Abigail was on a raft that overturned crossing the Big Blue. I had to stand within call of her and see her drowned."

"That's awful!"

Rebecca spoke so passionately it was an effort to remember these were lines she had rehearsed.

"Memories are nothing but pain to me now. I wish to forget, but I cannot. It is why I choose to slumber. And then you appear, waking me, and inquire after things best left forgotten."

I shook my head in admiration. "You're good! You really make me believe all those bad things."

"Why should you not, when they are true? And then I took sick myself."

"Wait, so you *are* sick?"

"I was. That morn, I reckoned I felt peevish from so much fatigue and vexation on our journey. And then came the gripes in my bowels. We had medicine— laudanum and camphor, physicking pills and castor oil. But none of it would do."

Rebecca tilted her head back. I gasped as her face came into view. Her eyes were sunk in gray hollows. Her whole face was barely skin over a skull. Even though she was a child, lines marked her forehead and bracketed her mouth.

But worst of all, her skin was an odd shade of gray-blue.

"Oh, Rebecca, you look awful. You need to go to the hospital or something."

"You think to gull me? I am hampered here. I

cannot move." She turned her head and tugged at something behind her.

I looked closer. A mist of rope even longer than her braids ran from the back of her head and disappeared into the floor.

I understood then, cold horror washing over me. Until now I had only seen dead animals above the spot where their bodies had been buried. "You're dead. You're already dead." I swallowed. "You must be buried here."

"I made Papa promise to bury me deep. How many graves have we seen dug up by wolves because they were too shallow?" She looked up, remembering. "That poor woman with a comb still in her hair. And a few days later, an arm lying in the wagon ruts. Just an arm. We never could find the grave from which it came."

"So your body is down there someplace." I pointed at the floor. "Underneath this building."

Rebecca nodded. "My papa said being dug out of one's grave was indeed a dreadful fate, but those who were departed no longer cared. Clearly, he was in error. But he did what I asked, even though it took two days. And I have not seen him since, nor any of my kin. Only strangers who have not deigned to answer me, no matter how many times I called. Until you."

She looked past my shoulder. I turned to follow her gaze.

Mrs. Whipple was standing behind me. And judging by her face, she had been there for quite a while.

"Adele, who are you talking to?" she said slowly. She edged toward me until one of her legs was in about the same spot Rebecca was already occupying. The two of them overlapped in ways that hurt my eyes and made my head ache. Rebecca wasn't quite as solid-looking as Mrs. Whipple.

"You have got yourself into a scrape," Rebecca observed. "You will not make her sensible I am here. I know, for I have tried to converse with people over the years, and you are the first to see me."

A needle of pain slipped into my temple. "Oh, I was just playing pretend," I ventured. But Mrs Whipple's expression didn't change.

Other girls had crowded in behind her. One of them was Tori. She pointed her index finger at her own head and spun it in circles.

Crazy.

CURSED

A few days after visiting the Oregon Trail museum, I was sitting on a brown leather couch, which didn't seem like something you'd find in a doctor's office. But then again, Dr. Duncan wasn't like any doctor I'd met before.

"So, Adele, your grandpa says that when you were at the museum, you were talking to someone from the Oregon Trail times." His voice was matter-of-fact. "I've spoken to other people who've had similar experiences, and I'm wondering what that's like for you."

Relief flooded me. So I wasn't alone.

Dr. Duncan was a psychiatrist. After Mrs. Whipple called my grandpa, he had driven me straight to my pediatrician, insisting I be seen immediately because I was hallucinating. When we were finally taken back to her office, she drew blood, weighed and measured me, listened to my heart, and sent me to a special room where they took pictures of my brain. But in between, she and my grandpa talked in low voices about my mom and my grandma and their problems. My mom's mom had died in a mental hospital. And even before my mom was killed in a car accident, she had lost her interest in living. After my dad died, she forgot to eat, forgot even to take care of me.

When all the tests on my body came back normal, I ended up at the psychiatrist's.

Unlike my pediatrician, Dr. Duncan didn't wear a white coat, but a pale blue shirt under a dark blue sweater. There was no judgment on his face. Instead he looked . . . interested. He leaned forward, his eyebrows raised, his expression open.

And I was so naive I thought he would believe me if I told the truth. He already knew it happened to others, so why wouldn't he? So I explained about Rebecca. How I had slowly come to realize she was dead, her bones buried under the museum.

He listened intently, without interrupting. When I finished, I sat back, feeling lighter.

"So this Rebecca, did she look real to you?"

"She *was* real. Just because other people couldn't see her didn't mean she wasn't real."

"Did it upset you when your teacher couldn't see her?"

I pressed my lips together for a second, remembering. "I saw the way Mrs. Whipple was looking at me. She looked scared."

"And have you seen other people like that girl before? People that other people couldn't see? People you thought had died?"

"Not people. Just animals." I told him about the dog in Pam's backyard, the bird in Tori's basement, the cat by the dumpsters.

Once at a restaurant, I had even seen a live fish floating in the air above its dead self. The one on the plate had been one of those fish cooked with the head still on. That was scary enough, the flat, dead silver eye. Everyone thought that was why I started crying. But it was really the second fish hovering in the air right above the first. A thread of mist bound their heads together.

As I talked, Dr. Duncan occasionally nodded or wrote down a word or two. It was a relief to finally tell the truth. I even repeated what my mom had said about it running in our family, though part of me wondered if I should be revealing her secrets. If keeping secrets still mattered when the person you had made the promise to was dead.

"And you say you see this little rope coming from the back of their heads if they're dead?"

"It's all misty-looking. It makes it so they can't go very far. They're tied to the head of the body they used to be in."

He sat back in his chair. "Well, you're lucky, then. My other patients who see things don't have a clue like that to tell them it's a hallucination."

"But it's not a hallucination. Rebecca was real." I had developed an explanation. "This kid in my class, Dylan, he's color-blind. He can't see pinks or reds. But just because he can't see those colors doesn't mean they aren't there. Maybe it's the same with the things I see. Everyone else is ghost-blind."

Dr. Duncan nodded, his face noncommittal. "I'm wondering if it might be a good idea not to tell other people about what you see."

"Why?"

"People can be unkind about things they don't understand. Even people who are your friends."

I nodded, thinking of Tori.

"I just have a few other questions I need to ask you." He leaned forward. "Do you ever think about hurting yourself?"

I pulled back. "No."

"Or hurting someone else?" Dr. Duncan's voice was blandly neutral, as if wanting to hurt other people was something we all did and just didn't talk about.

"No."

"Do you ever think you're being given a special message, or are supposed to do a special project, or that you've been selected to be someone special?"

"I guess," I said slowly. "I mean, most people can't see what I see. So maybe seeing the dead makes me special."

He pursed his lips. Had that been the wrong answer? "Do you think you're in danger, Adele?"

That was an easy one. "No." The dead couldn't hurt me. Once the dead kitten that hung out by the apartment dumpster had scratched me. I had felt the pressure of its claws, but when I looked down, there wasn't the faintest of marks.

"Do you ever hear voices from the TV or the radio when they're not on?"

"No." Seeing the dead made a rough kind of sense. Voices coming from the TV when it was turned off seemed like something that would only happen to someone who was mentally ill. Slowly, I was realizing I had made a mistake. A big one.

"Do you know what I am thinking now?" Dr. Duncan tilted his head and made his mouth smile. But to me it looked like he was just baring his teeth.

"Not really. I mean, I could guess." I was starting to get mad. Underneath the anger was fear. Because what was going to happen to me now?

"And what would you guess?"

"You think there's something wrong with my brain."

"That's not it at all, Adele." He shook his head, looking sad. "I think you have a disease. But it's not your fault. We all have circumstances occur that we need to overcome. This is yours."

"So you don't think Rebecca was real?"

"No." There wasn't a trace of doubt in his voice. "She wasn't. I'm going to give you some medication, but in the future, if you see someone or something that might be dead, ask yourself what the likelihood is that it's not real. And if others can't see what you are seeing, or if you see that silver rope, just note that you are experiencing a hallucination and move on. Don't interact with it. The more you act like it's real, the more weight you give it. Leave if you can. If you can't, ignore it. Keep busy to distract yourself. Don't attend to the hallucinations. In the long run, it's only hurtful." Dr. Duncan got to his feet. "I'm going to get your grandfather now."

Grandpa looked out of place in the office, which was decorated in shades of turquoise and dark brown. In his worn clothes, he sat next to me on the couch, rubbing his twisted hands.

"All of Adele's test results are normal, as Dr. Nelson probably told you," Dr. Duncan began. "She's a little taller than average for her age, a little thinner. Her blood pressure is great. Her blood tests were all within normal limits—no signs of alcohol or drugs, or chemical exposure, or an out-of-whack thyroid. No signs of a tumor on her scan. I haven't observed any delays in language or motor development. Her emotions are appropriate. You're not reporting any problems at school. These are all very good signs."

"But she sees things," Grandpa said between clenched teeth. "She sees dead people."

Dr. Duncan corrected him. "What she *perceives* to be dead people. Adele's a smart girl. She has a vivid imagination. But it's more than that. Using her imagination would be a choice. But this girl she thought she saw, this 'Rebecca'"—I heard the quotes in Dr. Duncan's voice—"that was something she perceived as being thrust upon her. You need to remember your granddaughter didn't choose this."

After a long moment, Grandpa said, "Then it's her mother's fault. She encouraged Adele to have these so-called visions. To pretend to see things just to get attention."

"No," I say, stung into speech. "She told me never to talk about them."

"It's good you brought her in," Dr. Duncan said, as if I hadn't spoken. "Adele is quite young, but given the family history, it's not surprising she's already displaying symptoms. Not only is there a genetic component, but her mother raised her to think that it was possible to see things that aren't really there. She told Adele to keep it a secret, which of course increased her fascination."

"Our family is cursed." Grandpa's fingers, stiff as claws, left furrows as he ran them through his hair. "And now history is repeating itself. Adele's mother, her grandmother—my daughter and my wife—all lost to delusions. I won't lose Adele too!"

"That's why it's good we're getting a handle on it now," Dr. Duncan said as he took out a prescription pad. "I'm going to put her on a medication that should cut back dramatically on the hallucinations, perhaps eliminate them altogether."

And then Grandpa squeezed my hand with one of his knobby ones. I could tell he was sure this was good news.

TUESDAY, NOVEMBER 27, 6:43 A.M.

SUPPRESSING THE TRUTH

can't move. A weight presses on my face, smothering me. My arms are pinned to my sides. My legs try to kick but barely stir.

I'm buried. Just like Tori.

I try to scream but don't make a sound.

And then I wake up with a gasp. I thrash free of the comforter that has wound itself around my body. I move the pillow from over my face to under my head.

After everything that happened last night, I barely slept. Talking to Tori. Uncovering the face of the dead girl she'd once been. Kissing Charlie. Deciding to start taking my pills again. Then seeing all the cops turning into the park, and flushing my pills.

I check the local news on my phone.

"Body Found in Gabriel Park" is the main headline. It doesn't give the person's name. But I know who it is.

So I wasn't mentally ill yesterday.

And I wasn't mentally ill when I talked to Rebecca in the bathroom of the Oregon Trail museum.

I've probably never been mentally ill.

And that must mean my mom wasn't either. Or my grandma.

All these years. All those pills. The doctors were wrong. My grandpa was wrong. The pills weren't suppressing delusions.

They were suppressing the truth.

But what about the other people I've seen or read about, the ones who don't take their meds? The ones who think their fillings are beaming messages at them, or the CIA is following them? The ones who put tinfoil over their windows or wander the streets in filthy clothes, muttering and shouting? The drugs they should be taking are the ones that stopped me from seeing the dead, so are those people also seeing something real?

I don't know. All I know is I'm not mentally ill.

But who's really going to believe me? If I try to tell anyone, it will probably just be seen as more proof that I *am* mentally ill.

Suddenly, sadness tinged with horror washes over me. No matter what, Tori is really dead. Despite everything that's happened between us, I never, ever would have wanted that.

And she was *murdered*. I sit up. Did Tori tell me anything that could help the police if they knew it? Is the fact that she doesn't remember her own death a clue?

Maybe that means the killer slipped a roofie in her drink and then strangled her. Or snuck up behind her, hit her on the head, and then finished her off once she was unconscious.

But there's no way I can tell the police anything she said. They would never believe me. I slump back. The autopsy should give them evidence, though, right? There must be clues on Tori's body. A hair from her murderer. Fingerprints. Fibers. DNA.

There's nothing I can do to help find her killer.

The only person I can help is me. And I definitely want to hold on to this feeling of being alive and awake. So I'll keep skipping my pills. And if I see anything or anyone that might be dead, I'll stay quiet, the way my mom told me to. It shouldn't even be hard. Other than roadkill or long-gone pets, how often am I ever near a dead body?

I get up and get dressed. In the breakfast nook, Grandpa is eating the same thing he does every day: generic shredded wheat topped with a sliced banana. He taps the newspaper with a gnarled finger.

"It says here they found a body in Gabriel Park."

"Really?" I widen my eyes. "What happened?"

"It doesn't say. But I heard a lot of sirens last night." He shakes his head, his gray eyes filled with worry. "I don't want you cutting through the park anymore. Not until they know what happened."

I have to leave ten minutes early so I have time to walk around the park instead of through it. As soon as I get on the bus, Marnie Martin waves me to where she's sitting. All the seats are taken, half filled with commuters and half with students. As we lurch forward, I grab the back of her seat for balance.

"Did you hear?" Marnie clutches my free arm. "Tori was murdered!"

"What?" The metal bar of the seat slides underneath my suddenly sweaty hand as we round a corner.

Her eyes gleam. She's like me, always on the edges, but now she's center stage. "They found her body last night in Gabriel Park!"

Aspen Wu leans across the aisle. "Don't talk to her, Marnie." She points at me. "Adele's the one Tori had to kick out of her party Saturday night."

Marnie shrinks away from me. Her features bunch together. "Adele? That doesn't even make sense."

Everyone is staring at me, even the adults. At the next stop, I push past people and leave through the back door. It's still a half mile to school, but I don't care.

Despite the chill, I'm sweating by the time I walk in the main doors. The halls are buzzing. The guys are talking in low voices, their jaws set, their hands balled into fists. Some of them look red-eyed. Most of the girls are full-out crying, their arms around each other. Sofia Reyes is sobbing in front of her locker, her mascara running down her cheeks in stripes. Next to her, Petra Khan has her mittened hands over her face.

Even the teachers are gathered in groups of two or three, shock on their faces. Mr. Hardy leans against the wall, one hand covering his eyes. He's the student teacher in language arts. Half the girls in school have crushes on him. Usually he could be mistaken for one of us, only with more elaborate facial hair, slightly nicer clothes, and a lanyard around his neck that holds his teacher ID card. Today he looks old, with gray skin and exhausted eyes.

A few feet from my locker, Jazzmin Walters and her boyfriend, Ethan Herrick, are talking in low voices. They were both at the party on Saturday. Usually I'm not on their radar, and today is no exception.

"But we left the party together," Jazzmin says. Her straight blond hair is held back by a narrow pink cloth headband. "And we didn't see anything."

"Right," Ethan agrees, pushing his coppery curls out of his eyes.

To my surprise, Jazzmin's blue eyes focus on me. She leans in close to Ethan and whispers, then glances back at me over her cupped hand.

She's not the only one looking at me. My stomach churns as I grab a book and slam my locker closed. For a second, I find myself wishing I was back on my meds, because then I wouldn't notice or care that people are staring.

But then something happens that makes everyone's head swivel. Luke Wheaten walks in. Tori's boyfriend. Except she said they broke up Saturday night. I can't imagine what he's going through. The last memory Luke will have is of her yelling at him. At least my memory is going to be of Tori weeping in my arms, begging me to help her.

He looks like a different guy from the one I saw at the party. His jaw is stubbled, his face hollow with grief. Normally his hair is swept back, but today it hangs over his shadowed eyes.

Just the sight of his reddened eyes is enough to make some girls start crying. For a second he's surrounded by respectful silence. Then the other football players, led by Murphy Lockhart and Justin Booth, move forward and surround him, like all the times they've huddled on the field.

"Man, I can't believe you're here," Murphy says, slinging his arm around Luke's neck.

The hall is so silent we can all hear Luke's response.

"Where else am I going to be?" His voice cracks. "I would rather be here than home by myself with nothing to do but think. Think about what some creep must have done to her." He holds up his hands and stares at them, turning them from side to side like he doesn't recognize them. "It's like a loop that won't stop."

Suddenly Luke pivots. With a roar, he shakes off Murphy's arm. He takes two steps and begins to hammer the sides of his clenched fists on the wall.

OUR FAULT

The bell rang as Murphy and a couple of other football players were trying to calm Luke. By that time, his hands already looked bruised.

As I take my seat in economics, the speaker on the wall crackles. It's time for the announcements, read each morning by two students chosen at random. But today the voice belongs to the school secretary. Mrs. Cox tells us to go to the auditorium for a schoolwide assembly.

Back in the hall, more people side-eye me, whispering to each other. And then behind me, I hear the hiss of a word. It's not a word I ever would have thought anyone would call me. And maybe they're not. Maybe I'm imagining it. Maybe they're talking about someone else.

In the auditorium, the teachers don't even try to be in control. Rather than being required to sit together by class, people wave and call to each other, even climbing over rows of seats to make sure they sit with friends. I find a seat near the front. Too late, I realize Charlie is in the row behind me, a few seats to one side. He opens his mouth and leans forward, like he wants to say something to me, but luckily he's too far away to talk to me.

A finger taps on the microphone. It's Ms. Chaudry, the principal. People settle down much faster than normal. All of us are hungry for news.

"As you may already have heard, one of our own was found dead in Gabriel Park last night. Tori Rasmussen." She pauses, swallows. "She was murdered."

A few girls wail dramatically, but for the most part, the auditorium is silent and still. No one is whispering. No one is nudging their neighbor. No one is looking down at their laps, checking their phones.

I surreptitiously glance at Luke. He's on the other side and farther back. He sits slumped, his chin on his chest and his left hand covering his eyes. I wonder if he's changed his mind about coming to school.

Ms. Chaudry continues, "Even though the police do not believe the murder occurred on school property, until they make an arrest, our first priority must be keeping all of you safe. I've asked our school resource officer, Jim Werdling, to talk to you about that."

As he steps up to the mic, Officer Werdling throws his shoulders back. He constantly roams the halls and the cafeteria, but I've never talked to him other than to echo one of his overly enthusiastic hellos. He looks like he's close to retirement, a short, gray-haired man with a small gut perched just above his belt. Even though he works at Wilson, he's a real cop. His utility belt carries a flashlight, handcuffs, a Taser—and a gun.

He clears his throat. "Driving here this morning, I passed a couple of young women jogging in the dark with their earbuds in." He shakes his head. "I saw both males and females walking alone in isolated areas. Or looking down at their phones because they were texting. They were not situationally aware of what was going on around them. They had no idea if someone was targeting them."

His message is clear. If any of us get ourselves murdered, it will be our fault.

"Make sure you are aware of your surroundings at all times. Don't go places alone, especially after dark. Whenever possible, travel in groups." He scans the audience. "And effective immediately, Wilson will no longer have an open campus at lunch."

A collective groan goes up. The campus is only technically open for juniors and seniors, but pretty much everyone can and does leave during lunch if they want. They grab a sandwich at Subway, hit the gas station convenience store across the street for junk food, or slip behind the bushes that edge the parking lot to smoke.

"Detective Mark Geiger from the Portland Police Bureau is going to tell you more about what the bureau is doing to find Tori's killer." Werdling beckons to one side of the stage. "Mark?" A man in a dark blue suit strides in from the left. A gold shield is clipped to his belt.

The detective has deep-set blue eyes and a shaved head that's got the hair version of a five-o'clock shadow.

His nose looks too wide and flat, like maybe it's been broken.

"I know you kids must be scared," he says. "Worried. But we are putting a lot of resources into this. And we will not rest until we have apprehended the person responsible. We don't know yet if this murder was premeditated or just a crime of opportunity—in other words, if Tori was just in the wrong place at the wrong time."

"What about a serial killer?" Dylan Borecki calls out.

At his words, I hear indrawn breaths. Girls clutch each other.

Geiger shakes his head. "Serial killers usually target vulnerable people who won't be missed, like those who are homeless or have mental illness. But we don't have any other open cases similar to this one. All of Portland's recent murders have been between people who knew each other, or killings over drugs or gang affiliation. Tori's murder doesn't fall into those last two categories."

I catch on. He thinks whoever killed Tori knew her.

Which means her killer could be sitting in this auditorium. Geiger's eyes flick from face to face. "That's where we need your help. If you saw anything suspicious, we want to hear about it. We understand there was a party at Tori's house Saturday while her parents were out of town. We need to talk to everyone who attended, as well as to anyone who might have seen Tori after ten P.M. on Saturday. Myself and Jim and some other officers will be in the school office today to talk to you."

There were at least seventy-five people at the party,

maybe more. I wonder how many will be eager to admit that to the cops.

As if hearing my thoughts, Geiger says, "We understand there may have been some behavior at that party that wasn't strictly legal. We're not concerned with that. We're only interested in finding whoever killed Tori Rasmussen."

At the thought of the stupid thing I did at the party, I shift on the hard wooden seat. It lets out a groan, and everyone's head turns. Like Luke, I put my hand over my eyes. I just want people to forget about what happened Saturday, but that seems more and more unlikely.

I barely hear the principal telling the crowd about how, in addition to the police, there are counselors everyone can talk to. About how Tori's family has said we are all invited for the visitation and funeral, both of which will take place in this very auditorium because it's the only venue big enough to hold the hundreds of people expected.

My face is flaming. I hope it doesn't show. The party. Oh God.

Someone is going to tell the police what I did at the party Saturday.

So that someone should be me.

ANYPLACE ELSE BUT HERE

Mrs. Cox finally notices me. The school office, which normally would be quiet at this time of day, is full of students. The chairs are all taken, so people are sitting on the floor. Some wait in silence, while others talk in whispers. A few weep quietly into crumpled tissues. The room is lined with a half-dozen doors leading to small offices. All those doors are shut, but from behind them come the low murmurs of voices urgent with emotion.

"Oh, hello there, Adele," Mrs. Cox says over her white-framed reading glasses. She prides herself on knowing the name of every student. As usual, she is dressed in velour. Today it's a teal tunic worn over black pants. She picks up a clipboard and pen. "Do you want to talk to one of the counselors?"

"Actually, I need to speak to the police." I try to keep my voice low, but the room goes still.

She tilts her head. "You do?"

I lean forward and whisper, "I was at the party."

Mrs. Cox blinks. Twice. Then she picks up a different clipboard. "Okay, I'll put down your name."

As she does, a tall, thin man with a badge clipped to his belt comes out of an office. With him is Charlie. We look at each other in mutual surprise. But when the cop claps his hand on Charlie's shoulder, I register how much they look like each other. Is this guy his dad?

Charlie touches my arm. "Can I talk to you about last night?"

His voice is a whisper, but we still attract curious glances. "Umm, okay," I say, wondering how I'm going to explain things to him. I'd rather never have the conversation. "But not now."

I find a spot along the wall and slide down to the floor, uncomfortably aware of how much space my body takes up. Laquanda Quinn, who is sitting on the other side of the room, nods, setting her silver earrings swinging. On one side of me are Jazzmin and Ethan. On the other is Aaron Lum. He's talking to Justin, both of them swearing about how messed up everything is.

"Tori was drinking," Ethan says softly to Jazzmin. "She didn't know what she was doing."

"But *you* did." Jazzmin turns away from him.

Was Tori drunk Saturday? Every time I saw her at the party, she had a glass in her hand, and half those times she was shouting, "Shots!" then tossing down her drink. But then again, she had seemed completely sober when she was screaming that she never wanted to see me again. She hadn't been slurring or staggering or anything.

And me? I drank enough on Saturday to do something stupid.

One by one, people come out of the offices, and other people get called in, and new people join those of us waiting. After about thirty minutes, a door on the left opens. Luke comes out, accompanied by Detective Geiger. Everyone stops talking. Luke's eyes are red and wet, and his lips are pressed into a thin white line. He keeps his head down, not making eye contact with anyone as he pushes open the door to the hall.

The detective takes the clipboard from Mrs. Cox and says, "Adele Meeker?"

After getting to my feet, I follow him into what is normally a vice principal's office. He sits behind the desk. I take one of the two straight-backed chairs in front of it.

"I'm going to take notes," Geiger says, "but is it okay if I also tape-record this?" A small silver recorder sits on the edge of the desk.

"Sure, I guess." What did Luke tell him about Saturday night? Does the detective already know what happened? I rub my damp hands on the knees of my jeans.

"Okay." He presses a button and then picks up a narrow notebook. "Today is November twenty-seventh, and this is Detective Geiger talking with Adele Meeker." He asks me my name, my date of birth, my address, my phone number.

"Okay, Adele. How long have you known Tori

Rasmussen? And can you tell me a little bit about your relationship with her?"

"I've known her since kindergarten. In grade school, we were pretty tight, but as we got older, we drifted apart."

He scribbles down what seems to be a single word. I wish I could see what he wrote.

"And before her death, how often on average would you say you saw or spoke to Tori?"

"I probably saw her every day at school, you know, in the hall or something. But we didn't talk that much."

"And how would you describe her?"

In my mind's eye, I see her laughing with a group of people, Luke's arm around her shoulders. "She has— had—a lot of friends. She was popular. But she was smart, too. And funny."

"You say she had a lot of friends. Did she have any enemies?"

I hesitate. There are lot of people like me, people Tori teased, or cut off, or ignored. "I can't think of anyone who would *kill* her." And even when Tori finally accepted that she was dead, there was no one she pointed the finger at.

Geiger taps his pen on his notebook. "Sometimes people can get pushed into doing something they never intended to. If emotions are running high, or if they are under the influence."

I nod, then realize I'm chewing on a fingernail. I pull my hand away from my mouth.

"Why do you think Tori was killed?"

"I have no idea."

"Was there anyone she was afraid of?"

That's easy. Tori wasn't afraid of anyone or anything. Except for being left alone in the woods forever. "No."

The detective makes another note. "If Tori were threatened, how do you think she would have reacted? Would she have fought back, or would she have tried to run away?"

Tori has always been fierce. I've seen her argue with teachers. And once she cussed out Justin, even though he towered over her. "Fought." But she didn't have a chance, did she? I wince, thinking of the scratches on her throat, the marks left by her own fingers when she tried and failed to stop herself from dying.

"What?" Geiger tilts his head.

"Nothing."

"You told Mrs. Cox you were at the party Saturday night?"

"Yeah." Here it comes.

"And did anything unusual happen at the party?" His expression is noncommittal. What did Luke say?

"Well, Tori asked me to go. That was unusual. Because like I said, we weren't that close anymore."

"Why do you think she asked you?"

"She was in a really good mood that day. It was after class, and she was telling everyone about how her parents were going to be out of town the Saturday after Thanksgiving and she was going to have a party. And then she looked at me and said, 'You should come, Adele.'"

I had felt so proud to be asked. It had felt like another part of my new life was falling into place.

"And how did Tori seem Saturday night?"

"Happy. They have a karaoke machine, and she was killing it." I half smile, remembering her exaggerated gestures. "And when she wasn't singing, she was dancing."

"Was she drinking or using drugs?" The detective's tone is matter-of-fact.

"Drinking. But she wasn't drunk. She didn't like girls who throw up or pass out. She said she could drink as much as Luke and still keep going."

"And Luke—he's her boyfriend?"

"Yes." We are circling closer and closer to the story I don't want to tell.

"Did anything else unusual happen at the party?" He knows. I can tell he knows.

"Tori and I—we had a fight."

"What was it about?" His voice is calm, almost bored.

"I kissed him. I kissed Luke. And then Tori found us. And she wasn't happy."

EASY THERE, TIGER

My hand trembled as I drew liner on my upper eyelid. Ten minutes earlier, Grandpa's friend had picked him up to go bowling. He wouldn't be back until midnight or later.

The old me didn't wear makeup. She never would have snuck out, never have gone to a party. But the new Adele was going to see what she'd been missing.

Maybe I could even be friends with Tori again. Sure, she'd done some mean things to me, but I remembered how close we'd been as kids. Occasionally I still saw flashes of the old Tori. Sometimes I even got the feeling that deep inside she was just as lonely as me.

I didn't want to waste time walking or waiting for a bus, so I rode my bike. At Tori's house, I hid it behind a hedge. Standing in the darkness, I unzipped my coat and flapped it, trying to cool down from the mostly uphill ride. As always, I was dressed in black, but tonight my mom's antique silver locket was on the outside of my shirt, not nestled against my skin.

The street was lined with cars. Tori's three-story house, angular and modern, sat back from the street. Through the windows, I could see dozens of people.

What was I doing here? No one had seen me yet. Maybe I should just get back on my bike and ride away.

"Adele?"

It was Luke. I hadn't noticed him leaning against a tree. In his hand was a red cup. The light was behind him, leaving his face in shadow, but I would have recognized his voice or silhouette anywhere.

My heart started beating faster than it had while I was riding my bike. "Oh, hey." Was Luke wondering why I was here? "Umm, Tori invited me."

"Hmm," Luke said, but I couldn't tell if it was in agreement or surprise. "Then we should get you a drink." He turned toward the house, and I followed.

We had gone to different elementary and middle schools, so Luke hadn't known me before high school. For people like him, I had always been the plump, quiet girl.

I had been afraid all eyes would be on me when I walked in, but the opposite turned out to be true. The music was pounding, and people were focused on what was right in front of them—their Solo cups of beer and their shouted conversations. Perversely, I suddenly wished a hush had fallen, that people had looked up to see me with Luke.

The only person who noticed was Laquanda. She was standing by herself, holding one of the ubiquitous red cups, a row of bracelets running up her arm. She raised one eyebrow, and I nodded back at her. I felt a tiny spike of joy. We weren't exactly friends. But now that I had more energy, now that I was awake, maybe we could be.

Luke showed me where to put my coat, so I added it to the pile draped over a chair. Then I followed him back to the crowded kitchen. The counter was littered with bottles and bags of tortilla chips that now contained mostly crumbs. On the floor a tub of ice held a stainless steel barrel. He filled a cup from the keg and handed it to me.

While the walls had been painted new colors and the couch we'd walked by wasn't the same one from a half dozen years ago, so much of Tori's house still felt like my home away from home. I knew the location of the four bathrooms. I was sure if I opened the freezer door, there would still be neat stacks of low-calorie frozen dinners, plus a hidden pint or two of Ben & Jerry's. Tori and I always ate them, knowing her mom wouldn't complain because the ice cream wasn't supposed to be there.

After taking the cup from Luke, I immediately drank half of it, trying not to wince at the sourness. My thoughts flicked to the basement. If I walked downstairs, would I still see the parakeet? But I didn't really want to know. I just wanted to be a normal girl at a normal party. Doing all the things I had missed out on for years. Like talking to a beautiful boy.

Only what should I talk about? "How'd you do on the test?" I asked, then wanted to kick myself. Luke didn't want to talk about our history class. But I couldn't imagine what he did want to talk about.

As I waited for his answer, I tried not to gawk, like how staring at a solar eclipse will ruin your eyes forever. Luke's own eyes were as green as a cat's. His jaw was square. His brows were horizontal lines that angled up at the ends. Lighter strands, left over from summer, threaded through his brown hair, which was swept straight back.

"Okay, I think—a B. Maybe an A minus." He smiled then, the right corner of his mouth lifting higher. "I just wish I'd been born a thousand years ago." His lips were shaped like a valentine. There was an extra dimple on the right side of his mouth.

"Why?"

He leaned closer, and my heart stilled. "Because then there would be a lot less to study for class."

It was kind of a stupid joke, but I didn't care. At all. I just laughed.

His gaze dropped. "I like your necklace."

"It's a locket." I touched it. "It's been in my family for a long time." When my grandpa told me my mom was gone, I hadn't believed him. Not until he handed me her locket.

Luke bent down to look at it. I sucked in my breath and then hoped he hadn't noticed. His thick fingers closed on it and lifted it. "It's heavy! And what's the design?"

"Mostly flowers. With a tiny bird in the center."

Luke thumbed the catch. On one side was a black-and-white photo of my grandma wearing a pearl choker and matching earrings. Her short black hair showed off her strong brows and high cheekbones. Around her shoulders was a white wrap or stole or some other piece of clothing no one wore anymore. She died when I was in the first grade, and by that time she didn't look anything like that picture.

On the other side was my mom. It was the only photo I had of her. My grandpa claimed he didn't have more. And he was probably telling the truth, because I'd looked.

In it, my mom had the same dark hair as her mom, the same heart-shaped face and deep-set eyes. She wore a black turtleneck and lipstick that set off the bow of her mouth.

Luke's eyes looked back and forth from the photos to me. "Whoever they are, you really look like them," he said.

"It's my mom and my grandma. They're both dead." It came out blunter than I had intended.

"I'm sorry." He gently closed the locket and then let it go. It thumped on my sternum. Inside my chest, my heart was beating just as hard. To hide my nervousness, I drained the rest of my beer.

Luke held out his hand for my empty cup and refilled it. "Easy there, tiger," he said as he handed it back.

I was so focused on Luke that it was a shock when Tori came up behind him and slipped her arm around his waist. "Just don't throw up, Adele! Especially on my mom's carpet. I can't stand girls who can't hold their liquor." She tugged Luke by the hand. "Come watch me. I want to sing!"

Not knowing what else to do, I followed the two of them into the living room. Tori pushed some buttons on a console, and the music changed to a driving beat and guitars, but no vocals. Then she grabbed up a cordless mic and began to sing that old Journey song about a small-town girl. She danced in place, shaking her hips, adding gestures and dramatic expressions. All eyes were on her. Including Luke's.

My second beer was mostly gone. My cheeks felt weird. Numb. I pressed them with my fingers. My skin seemed like it belonged to someone else. Maybe I had drunk too much. But the beer was also making me not care that Luke was Tori's boyfriend.

When the song was over, Tori bowed theatrically, rolling her hand in front of her. People shouted and whistled. I was right there with them, clapping so hard my hands hurt, the empty cup at my feet. The beer had freed me to remember that Tori was still pretty amazing. Then Jazzmin took the mic. She was more tentative, her voice cracking on the high notes. I went back to the kitchen to get another beer. As I filled my cup, I tilted it the way I'd seen Luke do it. Then I leaned against the wall and people-watched. I didn't know where Luke and Tori were, and I told myself I didn't care.

Dylan was telling a joke to Aspen and Petra. Aaron was talking to Sofia, who was sitting on the kitchen counter, drumming her bare heels on the cabinets underneath. Aaron only had eyes for her tanned legs.

Justin and Murphy were in one corner, fake fighting while a ring of guys watched. "You gotta stand bladed," Justin said, turning so that his left side was toward Murphy. "Makes you less of a target and makes your rear-hand punch stronger." He grinned. "And in a street fight, never be afraid to fight dirty." His fist suddenly tapped Murphy's throat. Even though it didn't look like Justin had hit him that hard, Murphy grunted and staggered back, his hands rising to his neck. He swallowed, his face contorted, and then tried to cover his pain with a smile.

Maybe everyone wore a mask, I thought. Maybe everyone had one self they showed the world, with a weaker, damaged person underneath.

About the time I finished my third beer, I realized I had to go to the bathroom. The one by the front door was in use, as was the one off Tori's parents' room. The bathroom on the second floor also had a closed door. I headed for the darkened third floor, where Tori's room and the guest room were.

I was leaving her bathroom when I heard a sniffle. In the darkness, I could barely make out a figure facedown on the bed.

It was Tori.

ALIVE AND KISSING

Was Tori crying?

I hesitated. "Are you okay?"

She rolled over. In the light from the hall, her eyes looked wet. "Sometimes I wonder if people really like me."

I ventured closer, and she patted the bed. I sat on the edge. "You have lots of friends." I said. "Just look at all the people who are here."

She rolled her eyes. "There's free beer and no adults. Anyone would show up for that kind of party. Even *you* came."

Now was not the time to point out she had invited me. "But even at school, you always have people around you."

"But it's not real." Her voice vibrated with intensity. "That's just people hanging together because they're more afraid of being alone. We never talk about the truth.

About how we really feel about anything. Like how I hate it when my parents are gone. How it makes me feel scared and sad."

"It does?" When I'd slept over during grade school, I'd seen the housekeeper and the nanny more than I had the Rasmussens. If I did catch a glimpse of them, Mr. Rasmussen was always in a suit, on his way to some place, the keys to his Lexus in his hand. Mrs. Rasmussen was dressed either in silk or in workout clothes cut to show off her slender body, and she, too, was always on her way out the door.

"I just need to be able to be honest with people." Tori sat up so that she was next to me, her feet dangling off the bed. "You know what I mean?"

I did know what she meant. How many times had I felt scared and sad myself? "Yeah," I started, "sometimes I feel like—"

But before I could say more, Tori slung her arm around my neck and kissed me on the cheek. "I knew you'd understand." Then she was on her feet and out of her room. As she started down the stairs, she called, "Okay, everyone! Time to play a game."

I followed more slowly. From the kitchen, I could hear her yelling, "But first, shots!" When I walked in, she was slamming an empty shot glass on the counter. She grinned. It was hard to believe she had been crying just a few minutes ago. "We're going to play hide-and-seek." She clapped her hands. "I'm going to count to fifty, and you're all going to have to find a place to hide."

Because it was Tori, no one argued.

She put her hands over her face and shouted, "One!"

Everyone scattered, leaping behind the couch or into a closet, ducking behind the full-length curtains. A few people went up the stairs, but they all stopped on the second floor. I went back to Tori's bedroom and opened her closet. It was twice the size of the one I had at home. It was full of clothes, not just on the hangers but also on the floor. I squeezed in.

I held my breath. Outside the closet I heard muffled footsteps. But from downstairs, Tori's faint voice was still counting. "Thirty-four, thirty-five, thirty-six . . ."

The closet door creaked open. "I'm already here," I whispered. "Find your own spot."

Instead of leaving, the other person pushed inside and then closed the door.

"Forty-eight, forty-nine, and fifty!" Tori shouted. "Ready or not, here I come."

"Too late," Luke whispered, moving closer. "Here, scoot back."

It suddenly seemed imperative we not get caught. But the space wasn't really big enough for both of us and all of Tori's clothes.

I shuffled backward in quiet increments, pushing past silk and velvet and wool. Luke followed me, matching me like a puzzle piece. And then I reached the wall.

I was tall, but Luke was taller. My left shoulder pressed just under his rib cage. The top of my head fit underneath his chin. His body seemed so much warmer than my own.

"Aha! Caught you!" Tori yelled in triumph, but her

voice was muted. It sounded like she was on the second floor.

"Shh . . ." Luke's whisper stirred the hairs on my neck. I turned my head another inch, until his rough cheek met mine. I could feel every individual hair scratching me.

I shifted again, but it only made us fit closer together. Then without making a conscious decision, I found my mouth suddenly pressed against his. We weren't making a sound, but it was like everything inside of me was singing and shouting. I was alive and kissing. Kissing Luke Wheaten. Under my hands, his shoulders were taut with muscle. My nose filled with his sharp smell that was at once familiar and not. His mouth tasted like beer.

I was so lost in touch and smell and taste that I didn't even hear the closet door open. The first I knew was Tori shouting, "What the hell? What the actual hell! I can't believe this!"

We sprung apart. My head was spinning. Luke turned away. He pushed past the clothes and out of the closet. I followed more slowly.

"What were you thinking?" Tori shouted two inches from my face as people began to flood into the room.

I didn't have an answer for her. Thinking had never entered into it. My body had acted without my mind getting involved at all.

"What's the matter, Tori?" Petra asked as she pushed into the already crowded room.

"I caught Adele kissing Luke in my closet!"

Heat climbed my neck. I wanted to disappear. I

wanted to sink into the floor. I wanted to never have been born. Instead I tried to explain. "It's not like that. I was hiding, and Luke tried to hide there, too. But there wasn't space for both of us. We had to squish together." Even to my ears it wasn't convincing. "It's not what you think."

Only it *was* what Tori thought. And it was all my fault.

"That's the best you can do?" Tori's cheeks were nearly as red as her hair.

"It was an accident, Tor." Luke's quiet voice was in sharp contrast to her shrillness.

"How could kissing be an accident!"

"I was whispering to Adele to be quiet, and when she turned her head, our lips kind of met for a second. It just happened." Even though Luke was mostly speaking the truth, it sounded like a lie.

"Right!" Tori rolled her eyes.

"Do you seriously think I would—" Luke stopped himself, but I completed the sentence in my head. *Kiss Adele. Kiss someone as colorless as Adele. As plump. As boring.*

"Things don't just *happen*." Tori's tone slid, sarcastic. "They happen because someone wants them to happen." She rounded on me. "You've always been jealous of me. Always. You used to be my friend. Now you're nothing. Both of you are nothing."

"Tori, you're drunk." Luke's voice was low and calm.

"Not drunk enough. Not so drunk I can't see the truth. I'm tired of your excuses."

"It was just for a second," Luke said patiently. "It was

an accident, and then it was over. You're the one I want, baby. It didn't mean anything."

My heart shriveled. Then it blinked out of existence. The kiss didn't mean anything. I didn't mean anything. It was an accident.

I had to make this stop. "Look, Tori, this is all my fault. I kissed Luke. He didn't even have a chance to say no."

Tori rounded on me. "You're pathetic. You've been making cow eyes at Luke all night. And then you throw yourself at him." For all her passion, her eyes were strangely vacant.

I realized I was running my fingers across my lips. I didn't know if I was trying to rub off the kiss or just remembering Luke's mouth against mine.

She shook her head. "Look at you. You really think *you* can take Luke away from me." Someone laughed in disbelief.

I looked at the ring of otherwise unsmiling faces. At Tori's angry one. And at Luke, who wasn't even looking at me.

And then I pushed past them all and ran down the stairs and out the front door, grabbing my coat along the way.

IN NO CONDITION

've just explained to Detective Geiger what happened at Tori's party. I didn't give him all the details, but he knows I kissed Luke and that Tori found us.

"So then what happened?" Geiger's tone is neutral.

"I left. Went downstairs, got on my bike, and rode straight home." I'm leaving out the part about having to walk my bike most of the way because I was crying so hard I couldn't see. The whole thing was a blur.

He makes another note. "And where was Tori when you left?"

"She was still upstairs, along with everyone else." Even outside, I'd been able to hear her shouting at Luke.

"Did you see anything unusual on your way home?"

"I don't think so." I had only been focused on myself, on how I had screwed up everything.

Geiger persists. "Maybe a car driving slowly past you,

or a driver who stared too long? Or a person you passed on the street?"

I shiver. Does he think I walked or biked right past Tori's killer? If so, why didn't they take me? Although the answer is obvious. Even a serial killer would have found me less than appealing.

Then I remember something. "Wait a minute. Tori's neighbor did come out and talk to me. Or at least he tried to. I didn't really want to talk to anyone right then."

I'd been so embarrassed and ashamed that I was barely managing to walk and push my bike. My only desire was to slink off as soon as possible. Go home and forget I had thought maybe I could be like everyone else.

Geiger looks up. "Which neighbor?"

"This old guy from next door. Mr. Conner. He used to always be out working in his garden whenever I went over to Tori's house. But I don't think he recognized me. I guess I was making some noise, and he was worried about me."

"Noise?" Was I wrong about the detective not judging me? Maybe he's punishing me by making me spell it out.

My cheeks feel hot. "I was crying. He asked if I was okay." My flush deepens as I think of how Mr. Conner had offered to drive me home, his voice soft, his head cocked to one side, the fingers of one hand playing with the ends of one of the bolo ties he always wore. When I told him I was going to ride my bike, he countered that I was in no condition to be riding and that my bike would easily fit in the back of his van. I still said no, mostly because I hadn't wanted to answer any questions about what had happened. Or worse yet, have to sit next to him while I hiccuped.

"And was your family home when you got back?"

"I just live with my grandpa. And he was out bowling."

"What time did he get home?"

"Around midnight." When Grandpa looked in on me, I pretended to be asleep. I kept still even when he kissed me on the forehead.

"And did you see Luke after you left the party?"

Does the detective mean that same night or later? Either way, the answer is the same. "Not until school yesterday." I take a breath. "So what did Luke tell you about the party?"

"That's not important, Adele. This is really a conversation between the two of us." He pushes a card across the vice principal's desk. "If you think of something you forgot to add, give me a call. Day or night, it doesn't matter."

TOO MUCH, TOO FAST

"*Chet has known Dwight since elementary school, but lately their friendship has been strained. When Dwight drinks on the weekends, he turns into a completely different person. He is belligerent and aggressive, and often gets into fights. But when Chet confronts Dwight about his behavior, Dwight says that it never happened. He doesn't seem to remember his actions at all. When Chet sees Dwight pound five beers in thirty minutes one Saturday night, he realizes how serious Dwight's problem is.*"

I finish reading aloud and look up from the textbook. Today our class is working on the alcohol unit. It comes before the drug unit and after the abstinence unit. Health class is a catchall for any possible way adults worry teens might get into trouble. It covers everything from firearms to food safety, and it's all pretty commonsense. I barely pay attention and still get As on every test.

Borka looks around the room. "So what should Chet do?" She's always trying to get a "discussion" going, but it never quite works. Recently she's resorted to having us read the various scenarios in the textbook aloud. At least I got one about drinking instead of STDs.

"I don't think Chet needs to do anything," Dylan offers with a smirk.

"And why is that?"

"Because this is obviously something that happened in 1950, and Chet and Dwight are probably dead now. I mean, what teenage guys are named Chet and Dwight?"

Everyone laughs. Even me.

Charlie is sitting between me and Dylan, and for a minute our eyes catch. He frowns, and I look away. Even though I promised to talk to him, I have been avoiding him, coming in late to class and leaving as soon as the bell rings.

I've also been trying to keep my head down, to not notice the stares and whispers. Now people know what happened and how I forced myself on Luke at Tori's party. And I've eavesdropped on the stories about what happened after I left. Tori told Luke she didn't want to see him again. He tried to reason with her, but she just ordered him out of the house. Then she partied with a vengeance—dirty dancing with some of the guys, even at one point dropping the straps on her dress and flashing everyone.

And then sometime after that, Tori disappeared. The only reason things aren't worse for me is that people are busy speculating about who might have killed her.

Now Borka sighs. "The names may sound old-fashioned, but the problems with drinking too much don't change. If you drink, it lowers your inhibitions. You might end up doing things you wouldn't normally do, like driving drunk or having unprotected sex."

"Duh—that's why people get drunk!" Dylan stage-whispers, to giggles.

Out of the corner of my eye, I see Charlie's disapproving face. He's not looking at Borka. He's looking at me. He must be thinking about me and Luke. Probably wondering if I was drunk when I kissed Luke. Which I definitely was. I switch my gaze to the white acoustic-tile ceiling. There's a pencil lodged right above Borka's head.

She soldiers on, reading from a printout. "Even walking is more risky if you've been drinking. In 2000, one third of pedestrians killed in traffic accidents were drunk. And if you drink a lot at one time, you could end up getting alcohol poisoning, which affects your involuntary reflexes. That includes the gag reflex and even breathing." She repeats the word for emphasis. "*Breathing!* In worst-case scenarios, alcohol poisoning can kill you. Every fall, there are sad stories about college freshmen who drink all night, go to bed, and never wake up. And in between being drunk and alcohol poisoning are blackouts."

So-and-so got blackout Saturday. I've heard that said a lot on Monday mornings. In the tellings, it's always amusing. Or at least interesting.

"And you don't need to be an alcoholic to experience blackouts," she continues. "All you have to do is drink too much too fast. If you gulp drinks or drink on an empty stomach, then your blood alcohol content goes up fast. And at some point your brain can't transfer short-term memories to long-term memory. Basically, after a blackout, you wake up and you can't remember what you said, where you were, what you did."

"I knew someone who blacked out, but she was just fun!" Aspen smiles. "She got up on a table and did this whole act, just like a stand-up comedian. Only the next day, she didn't remember anything about it."

"That might seem like fun, but what if she had ended up with some stranger who didn't have her best interests at heart?" Borka leans forward, eager to engage. "Or if she had gotten behind the wheel? When you're in a black-out, you could be doing anything from just talking to vandalizing a building. All because you were drunk and without any inhibitions, you decided it was a good idea. And then when you wake up the next day, you won't remember anything you said or did, because it never got stored in your hippocampus. You might even wake up someplace you don't recognize."

I read between the lines. When you wake up, it might be in a strange bed. With no memory of how you got there or even who you are with.

"During a blackout, only your short-term memory keeps working. And short-term memory is basically a two-minute loop." She points at Aspen. "That's why your friend could be funny and probably not even seem drunk, but she still might end up repeating the same jokes."

Judging by the murmurs around me, Borka's words aren't scaring anyone off.

"And if you have a high tolerance for alcohol, if you skip meals, if you're a woman—you have a much higher risk of blacking out."

"Just because you're a woman?" Brianna objects. "That's sexist!"

"It's not sexist, Brianna." Borka presses her lips together and shakes her head. "It's reality. Women don't metabolize alcohol as well as men do. And we have different levels of the enzymes that help the body process alcohol. If girls try to keep up with the guys, match them drink for drink, they can really get themselves into trouble."

What Borka is saying is making me look back. How much of that night do I remember? I remember drinking, talking to Luke, drinking, watching karaoke, drinking, hiding in Tori's closet, kissing Luke. Being discovered.

I remember looking in the bathroom mirror at home. Finding that all my carefully applied makeup was now underneath my eyes, making me look like the world's saddest raccoon. Throwing up in the bathroom sink, then washing away the evidence. Lying on my bed and feeling the world spin.

But I don't really remember much about going home. What if Tori followed me and caught up with me outside Gabriel Park? What if I snapped and killed her?

If you black out, you might do things you wouldn't normally do, like textbook Dwight getting in fights.

What if I did something bad that night and don't remember it? I drank those beers so fast, faster even than I would have water.

But if I killed her, I didn't mean to.

Can you go to prison for something you don't even remember doing?

SHOW A LITTLE BIT OF RESPECT

The line to get into Tori's viewing stretches down the hall, out the doors, and wraps around the parking lot, despite the rain. Visitation was supposed to last from six to eight, but the line still goes on forever behind me. Reporters aren't being let in. They've been corralled in a roped-off section of the parking lot, where they're trying to cajole people into being interviewed.

When I joined the line, I slipped between two groups of elderly women. Even now that I'm indoors, I leave the hood of my black raincoat up. Word has continued to spread about how I threw myself at Luke at Tori's party. I've taken to skipping lunch and hiding in a quiet corner of the library. Now as the line moves forward, I tug my black pants up yet again. When I was still taking my pills, they were too tight.

There's a bottleneck of black and navy at the auditorium door. Inside, the loudspeakers are broadcasting a song popular last summer, the lyrics about dying young. Back then, it was kind of sadly romantic. Now it's just awful.

We shuffle forward. I can't see the stage yet, but I can see the space below it. It holds professional portraits of the Rasmussen family, blown up to life-size. Bored of waiting, a little girl in a black velvet dress is running in circles around the easels.

As soon as I step inside, Tori starts waving her arms. "Adele! Adele!"

Her casket sits in the center of the stage. White and gold, it's like something for a Disney princess. The closed bottom half is smothered in white roses. The open top half showcases the dead Tori's head propped up on a satin pillow.

But the other Tori—the one who is, for want of a better word, "alive"—stands on the stage's edge, as far from her dead self as the rope of mist will allow. Beckoning.

But I can't just cut in front of everyone else. The line snakes down the right side of the auditorium. Just before the stage there's a small table with a box of tissues and a guest book. Charlie has just picked up the pen to sign his name. I duck my head, but luckily he doesn't check out the line behind him.

The line goes up the stairs and onto the stage, where there's a break about a dozen feet short of the coffin, allowing each person to privately pay their respects.

Right now, Aaron is leaning over Tori, his lips moving. On the far side of the stage, Mr. and Mrs. Rasmussen are exchanging a few words with Laquanda.

I scan the room for Luke. In scattered seats, people sit talking in small groups or crying alone, but I don't see him.

"Adele, come up here!" Tori demands. Even though she's at least a hundred feet away, her voice is clear as a bell.

I wish I were anyplace but here. A needle of pain slips into my temple. Can I answer her with only a thought? *Just wait a sec, Tori*. Her beckoning doesn't falter. I try a mental shout. *Tori!* No change. It's clear she can't hear my thoughts.

I bow my head and put my hands over my face as if overcome with emotion. "Can you hear me now?" I whisper lightly. With all the murmured conversations around me, I can't even hear myself. But Tori does.

"Yes! Finally. Come up here, Adele. It's horrible not being able to talk to anyone."

"I can't do that," I whisper. "I have to wait my turn."

She makes a pouty snort. "Okay, whatever."

Behind her, Maddy D and Maddy P approach the coffin together, their arms around each other.

No one is paying attention to me, so this time I only cover my mouth. "The police have been interviewing everyone who was at your house. Don't you remember *anything* about what happened?"

"I told you, the last thing I remember is being at the party."

"Look at that," an old lady says behind me. I freeze.

"What?" a second old lady says.

"That girl's in a halter top!"

"Shh!" one of their equally elderly friends whispers.

For a confused second, I think they're talking about Tori, but then I see they mean Sofia. She's dressed in black, but her shirt ties behind her neck, leaving her shoulders bare.

The first old lady continues, "You better believe I am biting my tongue. That is a dead person and their grieving family up there. Show a little bit of respect! But no, it's all jeans and polo shirts and halter tops."

She's not wrong. Half of my classmates are in formal clothes—most of the guys look uncomfortable—and the other half wear outfits better suited for a trip to Home Depot.

Onstage, Charlie, dressed in a suit that's too big, is now standing over the coffin. His hands are clasped in front of him, and his head is down. I think he's praying. Murphy is next in line. In dress pants two inches too short, he shifts from foot to foot. Is he nervous because he feels guilty? Because he knows something? Or because—and this seems more likely—it's the first time he's been near a dead body? After Charlie leaves, he walks up to the coffin.

"I'm right here, Murphy," Tori shouts in his ear. He doesn't flinch, just stands there looking down, his face stoic and yet somehow scared.

"See?" Tori turns back to me. "This is driving me up the wall. I hate being able to see people and have them not see or hear me. And watch this!" She grits her teeth like she's about to pick up something heavy. Instead she rests her fist on Murphy's back. With a grunt, she begins to push. Her fist slowly disappears without distorting Murphy's flesh or, as far as I can tell, making any impression on him at all.

He finally raises his head and turns toward Tori's parents. As he does, her arm slips out of his side. She opens and closes her fingers stiffly.

"How'd you do that?"

"I have no idea. It's not easy. But I can go through things if I try hard enough. People. Objects. I even went into a different room at the funeral home. It'd be cool except I can't actually go very far because of this stupid tether." She reaches behind her and tugs at it.

So the stories get part of it right. Ghosts can move through walls. "How'd you figure it out?"

"The first time must have been in that grave, but I don't remember it. Now it's just a way to pass the time."

Justin's up next. He leans down.

"He kissed me!" Tori's voice is equal parts repulsed and pleased. "And he gave me one of those airline liquor bottles. A lot of people are leaving notes and stuff. I wish I could read what they say."

The liquor reminds me of Tori shouting, "Shots!" at the party. A piece of the puzzle suddenly falls into place. No wonder she doesn't remember being killed. If anyone blacked out that night, it was Tori. Not me.

Covering my mouth again, I whisper, "How much did you have to drink that night, Tori?"

She puts her hands on her hips. "Are you saying it's my fault I got killed?"

"No. But it could explain why you can't remember. When you black out, you can't form memories."

"I assure you, I can hold my liquor," Tori says as her elderly neighbor Mr. Conner, the one who wanted to give me a ride, leans over her coffin. "Yuck." She makes a face as the ends of his bolo tie dangle an inch from the dead Tori's face. "He's so gross. Every time I sunbathe in the backyard, he's out pretending to water his plants. Wearing sunglasses, like I won't be able to tell he's staring. Sometimes I like to mess with him. You know, untie my top so I won't have a tan line and watch what happens to his face. Even behind sunglasses you can tell his eyes are bugging out."

"He wanted to give me a ride that night," I whisper into my cupped hand. In light of what Tori just told me, his offer seems far creepier than it did a week ago. "And he didn't want to take no for an answer."

Straightening up, Mr. Conner adjusts his bolo tie before he starts toward the Rasmussens. The tie is black, made of leather or cord. My mind flashes back to the red furrow around Tori's throat.

What if he took that tie off his own neck and slipped it over hers?

YOU HAVE TO TELL THEM

Mr. Conner is shaking hands with Tori's parents. Am I looking at a killer? From here, he seems more pathetic than anything else.

But maybe those are the ones you have to watch out for.

Soon I'm climbing the stairs and then it's my turn to walk to the casket. I keep my eyes on my feet so the Rasmussens don't catch me staring at the live version of their daughter.

Inside the coffin lies what appears to be a wax sculpture of Tori. Plastic and unreal. Her eyes are shut. Her mouth is neither smiling nor frowning, but her lips sag back in a way that makes it obvious she's not simply asleep.

She's dressed in a white blouse with a high, lacy neck. Underneath is a faint shadow. I look closer. Through the lace, I see a tan bandage wrapped around her neck, covering the line where she was strangled. A bandage on a dead body. What's the point? They can't fix her now.

But maybe it felt like they had to try.

Her hands, looking oddly translucent, lie one on top of the other in a pious position the real Tori would never take. Tucked around her body are a half-dozen handwritten notes, as well as cards in sealed envelopes, a tiny Moonstruck Chocolates box, and that airline bottle of liquor Justin left.

"So how do I look?" Tori asks from next to me. Her voice trembles a little.

Someone has carefully done her makeup. I wonder how hard it is to put mascara on a corpse. Her hair still bears the marks of the curling iron.

I lean closer like I'm whispering something into the dead Tori's ear rather than talking to the girl standing next to me.

I lie. "You look good." Then I inhale and gag. They must have done something to the body to preserve it. It smells awful, a sort of plastic, fishy smell.

"Be honest, Adele." Tori makes a sound like a laugh. "The lady at the funeral home did a terrible job. It was like I was this life-size doll and she was playing with it. I just had to sit there and watch. I tried to tell her I would never wear that color eyeshadow, but she didn't even blink. Finally, I turned my back and went as far away as I could."

"So can you ignore what happens to your body?" I whisper.

"Not totally. I mean, I can't feel anything that happens to it, but I'm still tied to it. Literally." The rope of mist slithers underneath the dead girl's head. Tori shivers. "I couldn't leave when they did the autopsy either."

"Oh my God." I press two fingers against my temple to counteract the pain.

"If there had been a wall close enough, I would have pushed through it and stood on the other side. But there wasn't. So I had to watch them cut me open and then crack my ribs apart." She swallows. "And worse."

Even though it feels useless, I say, "I'm sorry."

"I just tried to go to sleep."

"You still sleep?"

"That's not exactly it, but close. Most of the time, I just close my eyes and it's like I'm nothing and nowhere. But being around you wakes me up somehow."

Out of the corner of my eye, I see the old lady next in line glaring at me. "I can't stay here any longer, Tori. People are waiting."

"Okay, but stick around after you talk to my parents." Murmurs fill the auditorium behind us. Tori gasps. "Luke's here!"

Luke is joining the Rasmussens. I've never seen him in a suit before. The dark blue contrasts with his pale, shadowed face. Around his neck is a gray bow tie. Until now I imagined bow ties being for old men, but on him it's elegant. "And you haven't seen Luke since—"

"Not since the party." She swears, her voice breaking. "Oh God, I just want to talk to him so bad. I already tried with my dad in the funeral home. He couldn't hear me at all. But maybe Luke could if I was close enough."

"Maybe," I say noncommittally.

"If I can't, you have to tell him I'm still alive."

"That's the kind of thing that got me diagnosed as schizophrenic." It feels too cruel to point out that being alive to only one person is not the same as actually *being* alive.

I straighten up and walk toward the three of them. Luke's eyes are glassy. Mrs. Rasmussen's face is drawn to the point of gauntness. Only Mr. Rasmussen seems unchanged, still dapper in a tailored charcoal suit, his face expressionless.

I don't know what to say. I settle for "I'm so, so sorry for your loss."

Mrs. Rasmussen hugs me. It's like being hugged by a broken bundle of sticks. She pulls back. "Hello, Adele. I haven't seen you"—she pauses—"for a long time."

From behind me, Tori says, "You have to tell them I love them."

I come as close as I can. "I know how much Tori loved you guys."

Instead of looking comforted, their faces, even Mr. Rasmussen's, register pain.

"How does she look?" Luke asks me. His voice is high and strained. "I haven't been able to . . ." Gesturing toward the coffin, he drops his head.

"She looks . . . good. Peaceful." I glance over my shoulder. Tori's arms reach out toward us, toward Luke, but she's at the limit of her tether.

He blinks, and a tear rolls down his face.

I look from him to the coffin. "I can go up there with you, if you want."

"Can you stand between me and"—he gestures out at the people in the auditorium, all of them watching us now—"and them? I just want to say goodbye."

A murmur sweeps the auditorium as we go back together to the coffin. Even with my hood up, people now recognize me. My back to them, I stand between them and Luke and the coffin with its dead Tori.

The living Tori becomes frantic. She strokes Luke's arms, his face. She hugs him. I close my eyes, not just because of that, but because of the naked pain on both their faces.

"Luke, it's me. Tori! I'm right here, baby. Luke. Oh, Luke!" She's starting to cry. "Can't you tell I'm here?"

Luke's whisper is so soft I can barely hear it. "Oh God, Tori, I wish, I wish everything could be different. I wish . . ." His words trail off, and I hear the tears come.

When I open my eyes, he is hugging the dead Tori. The idea of her cold, rubbery flesh, that smell of plastic and rotting fish, makes me feel even sicker. And maybe it freaks him out, too, because he quickly lets go, straightens up, and thrusts his fists in his pockets.

The other Tori stands next to him, her eyes closed, her mouth open, her chest heaving, with only me to witness her tearless grief.

With only me to know she exists at all.

YOU HAVE ONE THING

Together Luke and I walk back to Tori's parents. Tori goes as far as she can. Behind us, a new person takes our place. I leave Luke with the Rasmussens and walk down the steps. Ahead of me, I see a tall, thin figure in a too-big suit leaving the auditorium. Charlie.

"Please don't go, Adele," Tori says in a voice choked with tears.

Despite the headache that is now like a drill chewing through my temple, I do as she asks. Besides, the longer I stay here, the less chance that I'll have to interact with Charlie. I find a spot in the back of the auditorium, surrounded by empty seats, where hopefully my muttering won't be overheard. Tori has moved back to the head of the casket, but she's looking right at me.

"So if you can talk to the dead, what do they say happens next?"

Propping my elbow on the armrest, I hide my mouth with my hand. "You and that girl in the Trail Museum, you're the only dead people I've talked to. And it sounded like she mostly just slept, or whatever you call it."

What I tell Tori is true, as far as it goes. It's also true that before I started taking my medication, there were a few times my grandpa drove me past cemeteries. At the one closest to my house, I would always see an old man wearing a hospital gown emerge from a single grave near the fence. But once at a different cemetery in an old part of town, I glimpsed dozens of people pulling themselves out of their graves. Some of them had been so damaged at the moment of death that I slammed my eyes shut rather than see their gaping wounds and missing limbs.

But even with my eyes closed, I could feel their loneliness tugging at me. My hope was when there was no one like me around, they just slept. And that they didn't find themselves yanked back to life very often.

"My mom never came to see me in the funeral home," Tori says. "Just my dad." Her words hitch. "He was crying."

"Your dad?" It's hard to imagine. Her dad has always looked the same. Distant. A little disdainful. Even today.

"Not just crying. Sobbing. He kept saying he was sorry. Telling me if he could just turn back the clock, do things over, then everything would be different." Sadness colors her voice. "Only it was too late. Because back when I was alive, it didn't matter if I got good grades or flunked a class. It didn't matter if I came home late or never came home at all. I was always looking for a reaction, and I never got one." She attempts a smile. "Now they finally realize they have a daughter. But it's too late."

While we've been talking, Mrs. Rasmussen has been hugging every single person who has just walked past her dead daughter. Mr. Rasmussen shakes their hands. In between, he just keeps staring at the coffin, at the top of Tori's head resting on that tufted pillow.

And then there's Luke. Even this far away, I can see how sad his eyes are.

My attention is caught by a tall, thin man with a tired face scanning the auditorium. He wears a wrinkled blue suit. It's the guy I saw talking to Charlie in the school office, the one who looks like Charlie. The one who's a cop.

He must be here to figure out if one of Tori's mourners is also her killer.

"I know you don't remember who killed you, but has seeing anyone tonight jogged your memory?"

"No!" She makes a face. "I mean, I saw you looking at Mr. Conner, but he's just pathetic. And he's super old!"

"The police seem to think that it's someone you knew. Has anyone said anything that might be a clue?"

She shakes her head. "A few people have said mean things, that's all. I thought you weren't supposed to speak ill of the dead."

"Like what?"

"Aaron said, 'Sorry, Tori.' But he said it all sarcastic. And right to my face."

"He didn't think you could hear him," I remind her, pressing my temple with the tips of my fingers as if I could push the pain back in. "Besides, you did tell people he looked like a ferret."

"Well, he does!" she says, and I don't argue. With his prominent, pointy nose, she's right.

"Still, you have to admit that you did turn into kind of a bully as you got older."

"No, I didn't!" She blows air through pursed lips. "It's not like I was giving people wedgies or tripping them in the hall."

"You did it another way—made fun of people, sometimes to their face."

"I did not!"

"Not true. You made fun of Murphy because he always wears pants that are too short. And remember when you made an *O* with one hand and held it up to your eye like a sailor looking through a telescope? Then you yelled, 'Land ho!' when Maddy D came into the cafeteria."

Tori stops protesting. But I don't stop whispering. For years, I've been keeping track of things she's done.

"And you spread rumors about people. Or sometimes you just downright ignored them. You might not ever have laid a hand on them, but it still hurts when someone acts like you're not even there."

"Yeah, well, now I know exactly what that's like." Her mouth twists. "Maybe God has a sense of humor." Then she looks straight into my eyes. "I know why you can see me. It's because it's up to you to figure out who killed me."

"That's not why, Tori. It's just something that runs in my family."

"But you owe me," she insists, her lower lip jutting out. "If you hadn't come to my party, if you hadn't kissed Luke, then we wouldn't have fought. And I wouldn't have left. And whoever killed me couldn't have gotten to me."

"And what am I supposed to do that the real cops can't? They've got profilers and databases and search warrants. I'm just a high school student."

"For one thing, you're good at watching. Even when we were little, you always noticed things. Like when Mrs. Haslet"—she was our second-grade teacher—"stopped wearing her wedding ring. You noticed it right off."

I raise one shoulder in a shrug. "That still doesn't make me a detective."

"But you have one thing the real cops don't," Tori says.

"And what's that?"

She points at her chest. "Me."

SNAPPED

Tori wants me to team up with her. To sleuth. To unmask her killer.

"Okay, okay, I'll try." My right eye is watering. "But I have to go now."

Tori's eyes widen. "No! You can't go. You can't leave me alone."

"But I have to leave sometime," I point out. "Besides, what if while we're talking you're missing an important clue?"

Hope lights her face. "Maybe if they arrest the person who killed me, I'll be free. I'll be able to go on to whatever's next."

I don't point out that the girl at the End of the Trail museum hadn't been murdered, yet she was still stuck there 150 years later, just a little faded. I only nod. "You've got the best chance of anyone of figuring it out."

I stop whispering, because Aspen and Brianna are walking up the aisle near me.

"She kind of looks like she's sleeping," Brianna says.

"No, she doesn't." Aspen shakes her head. "She looks like she's dead."

As soon as they are past, I say, "I have to leave now, Tori. I'm sorry."

"But you'll come back tomorrow for the funeral? We can compare notes."

"Okay." I'm already getting to my feet. "Of course." My head is throbbing with every beat of my heart.

With my right eye closed, I make my way out of the auditorium. Every step away from Tori, the pain eases a notch. As I push open the heavy door, the fresh, damp air wakes me up like a splash of cold water.

It's a relief to be out of her sight. Out of earshot. Out here, Tori's really dead, not sort of alive. The pain continues to recede.

People are crowded outside the doors and clustered in the nearby parking lot. A few are talking to the reporters penned up on the far side. Cigarette and even pot smoke lingers in the air, and a few of my classmates are tipping back flasks I'm pretty sure hold more than just water. Out here, there's tears, of course, but there's also a few smiles and even a little flirtation. Tori belongs here far more than she does inside, where there's no one to flirt with and nothing to laugh about.

And out here, the idea that I can help Tori figure out who killed her seems more than slightly ridiculous. Despite what the police think, it probably was a stranger, some man who spotted her storming off and then took advantage of her being too drunk to realize what was happening.

As I wind through the crowd on my way to the bus stop, I overhear snatches of conversation.

"I heard she was stabbed to death," Aaron says.

"No, she was shot," Dylan declares.

Suddenly Petra is in front of me, blocking my path. "I can't believe you have the guts to show up here. It's your fault Tori's dead." Around us, conversation stills. "If you hadn't kissed Luke, he and Tori wouldn't have gotten into a fight, and she wouldn't have taken off." It's Tori's argument.

I swallow hard. "I was drunk, and I made a mistake. I wasn't thinking. Obviously." My breath shakes. "If I could apologize to her, I would. A million times." In truth, so far I haven't said it once. "And it's not like we were *never* friends. Tori and I—you know how close we used to be back at Maplewood."

"Yeah, like, when we were seven!" Still, Petra nods, appearing slightly mollified.

"I feel awful about what happened. That's why I came tonight."

"You *should* feel awful." But Petra's words lack their former vehemence. People turn away, losing interest.

"I'm not the one who killed her. Tori was just in the wrong place at the wrong time." My words make it sound like a mistake, an accident, as if she and the killer are equally innocent—or guilty. "So what happened at the party after I left?" I burrow my cold hands into my pockets.

"She told Luke she didn't want to see him again. That it was over between them. He tried to calm her down, but she just pushed him away and told him to leave. So he did."

That part I already knew. "And Tori? What did she do then?"

"You know Tori!" Petra rolls her eyes fondly. "She wanted everyone to think she was fine. She was dirty dancing. Singing karaoke. Getting people to do shots."

I nod. It sounds like Tori. And it also sounds like she wasn't exactly hurting.

The smile falls from Petra's face like a plate from a shelf. "When the party started breaking up, I couldn't find her, even though I looked all over. Sometimes when she drinks that hard, she does weird things. Once after a party at my house, I found her sleeping on my dog's bed."

Vintage Tori. Even a dog wasn't safe around her when she wanted something.

"While I was looking for her, her dad showed up. He wasn't supposed to be back until the next day. When he saw what was happening, he started yelling. I'd never seen him like that. He put his suitcase down and then he took his arm, and he just swept everything on the kitchen counter onto the floor." Petra demonstrates, swinging her arm in front of her. "Glass was breaking and everything. And he was grabbing at people, saying he was going to call the police. Everyone scattered. I ran out, too." She takes a deep, shaky breath. "And I never saw Tori again."

A chill runs across my skin that has nothing to do with the cold. What had Tori said? That in the funeral home her dad had cried and cried, repeating that he was sorry?

But what was he sorry *for*?

Was it for ignoring her when she was growing up? Or was it for something else?

In my mind's eye, I picture her house. In every room, something that could be the murder weapon, that could fit into that terrible red groove around Tori's neck. Electric cords on appliances. The cords on the custom blinds. Even kitchen twine.

Maybe the reason Mr. Rasmussen sobbed in the funeral home was because he had snapped. He had snapped and killed his own daughter.

SOMEONE WE KNOW

When Justin calls Petra's name, she leaves without saying anything more to me, not even goodbye. She just gives me one last side-eye and walks away.

As the ramifications of what Petra said wash over me, I start to shake. If Tori's dad is the one who killed her, would Tori really want to know? Right now, she's got some measure of closure, a feeling he's finally regretted the kind of father he's been.

I scrub my face with my hands. When I let them drop, I notice Laquanda leaning against a tree about fifteen feet away, smoking a cigarette. It's pretty clear she heard every word Petra and I said.

I walk over to her. "Can I bum one?" I don't smoke, but it gives me a reason to talk to her. Like me, Laquanda watches people. So what did she notice at the party that night?

She doesn't say anything, just pulls a pack from her purse. Silver rings glint on every finger and even her thumb. Then, when it's obvious I don't have matches or anything, she produces a lighter.

The first drag is bitter on my tongue and scratches my throat, but I refuse to cough.

"You were still at the party when I left," I say. I remember her watching, face impassive, while Tori berated me. "What happened after that?"

"When you *left*?" She snorts two streams of smoke. "Is that how you're telling the story? That you just decided for no reason to take off? Tori shamed you in front of everyone and then she practically marched you out of the house."

I keep my voice low. "That was my fault. Because of what happened with Luke." Just the thought of it makes the back of my neck hot.

"And Tori chose to handle it by dragging everyone else up there so they could witness her humiliating you. Now even people who weren't at the party know what happened." Laquanda leans closer. "And you should know they're all starting to talk."

"About how I kissed Luke?" The flush spreads to my face.

Her mouth twists. "About how you might be the one who killed her."

"That's ridiculous," I scoff, but her expression doesn't change. "Maybe I was upset, but there's no way I killed Tori. She humiliated a lot of people, not just me." I look closer at Laquanda's face. "What about you?" I ask, suddenly bold. "Did she ever make fun of you?"

She looks away. "No."

"*Right.*" I give the word a sarcastic spin. Even though I've never witnessed Tori mocking her, I know the truth in my bones.

"Okay." The words rush out of her. "She used to call me 'daughter of the night,' because I'm so dark. And she wouldn't stop talking about my hair, asking if she could touch it." Laquanda shakes her head of tight curls.

Count on Tori to say something outrageous. Or several somethings. "Then why were you even at her party? And why are you here?"

Her dark eyes meet mine. "Couldn't I ask you the same questions? You and I both know Tori is—was—complicated. She's smart. And funny. She could be generous. And it was impossible to take your eyes off her. She was like a force of nature. Sometimes you just want to be a part of that."

Her words set off echoes. Even when we were kids, it was hard to look away from Tori. I remember her making up elaborate stories about her Barbies. Telling jokes in class that made even the teachers laugh. And more recently, falling apart in my arms when she realized she was dead.

"That's Tori," I agree.

"Right. That's Tori. Which means she could also be cruel. And maybe one of those times is what got her killed."

"What happened at the party after I left? I heard she made Luke leave."

"After that, it was like she wanted to prove she didn't care. She was all over Ethan, and he's been with Jazzmin since middle school." Laquanda looks around before adding, "And Jazzmin was pissed about that."

I freeze, the cigarette halfway to my mouth. Jazzmin always wears cloth headbands. Headbands about the width of the mark on Tori's throat. I imagine Jazzmin looping one over her hands and then yanking it over Tori's head.

Reading my expression, Laquanda rolls her eyes. "Don't tell me you think Jazzmin could have gone after her. That skinny little track girl? Tori was so fierce. She would have decked her."

Laquanda doesn't know how Tori was killed, but I do. And according to what I found on the internet, it wouldn't take muscles or even much time. Compress the carotid arteries on the sides of the neck, and unconsciousness results in only ten to fifteen seconds. As one forensics site said, "The victim's death can come very suddenly after." I've tried to forget the pictures I also saw online.

I shrug. "I don't think it's that far-fetched. Not if she was mad. Maybe she snuck up on her."

"What about Ethan?" Laquanda counters. "Maybe he figured out Tori was just playing him to make herself feel better."

In my mind's eye, I see Ethan, his left arm permanently glued to Jazzmin's shoulders. Around his wrist, he always wears a woven black survival bracelet. I heard him talking once about how it's made of paracord. Which, according to him, can be used to make a shelter, a trip-wire, a tourniquet, and a million other things.

Or, I think, *a garrote to compress the blood vessels on the sides of the neck.*

"Did you see Tori leave the party?" I ask. "Did Ethan go with her?"

"What are you, the police now?" Her mouth purses. "Like I told *them*, I didn't see where Tori went. I didn't even know she was gone. I'd been talking to Murphy for a while, and then when I went back to the kitchen to get more beer, I realized a lot of people had already left. And then Tori's dad showed up and everyone took off. Including me."

Suddenly it hits me how ridiculous this all is. There's no way Ethan, Jazzmin, Tori's own father, or even creepy Mr. Conner killed her. Despite what the police think, it has to have been some stranger, some serial killer.

"Do you really believe the person who did this was someone we know?"

Instead of answering directly, Laquanda says, "Did you ever read that Agatha Christie book—and it was a movie, too, maybe a couple of movies—called *Murder on the Orient Express*?"

I shake my head.

"This guy is murdered on a train. The detective knows it has to have been one of the other passengers. Then it turns out every single person on the train had some kind of reason to kill him." She looks at me with eyes as dark as ink. "Maybe Tori's like that."

SIGNS OF A STRUGGLE

Laquanda throws her cigarette butt down on the wet pavement, then twists the toe of one of her Vans on top of it. She lifts her chin. "I gotta go."

"See you," I say, and I mean it. I feel like I'm really seeing her. I've talked to her more in the last few minutes than I ever have. Maybe when this is all over, we really can be friends, the way I first thought at the party.

She leaves me plenty to think about. Did Tori send Jazzmin into a jealous rage? Or did Ethan realize he was just Tori's plaything and decide to teach her a lesson? Or is Laquanda right, that it might be easier to make a list of people who *didn't* have a reason to be angry at Tori?

Lost in thought, I don't hear anyone approach. Then a voice next to me makes me jump. I let out an involuntary cry.

"I didn't realize you and Tori were that close." It's

Charlie. He's wearing a too-big black suit plus a white shirt and black tie. He looks like a Mormon missionary.

"What do you mean?" I'm hoping my shriek wasn't as loud as it sounded. At least the crowd in the parking lot has thinned out.

Charlie reaches out and wipes his index finger over my right cheek. "You're crying."

I flinch at his touch. My eye must still be watering, even though the headache has now faded into the background.

"Oh, now you don't want me touching you." He presses his lips together into a thin line, opening them long enough to add, "But it's okay if you kiss me in front of your grandpa. And then tell him we'd been studying in the laundry room. In a way that made him think we were doing a lot more than that."

"How do you know that?"

"Because he cornered me the next day and told me to stay away from you. He said you had *issues*."

I freeze. "What did you say?"

"I didn't say anything. He didn't give me a chance to. Trust me, this was definitely a one-way conversation." Charlie's voice sounds strangled. "What are you doing, Adele? Lying about me and"—he looks at his feet—"kissing me? You did that as soon as your grandpa opened the front door. The principle of Occam's razor says the simplest possible explanation is the true one. So I figure you must have been doing something you didn't want your grandpa to know about. And you distracted him by kissing me."

I wait for him to add something about me kissing Luke at the party, but he doesn't. Mentally, I cross my fingers and hope he never finds out.

"I just didn't need my grandpa grilling me about where I was." I'm not going to tell Charlie I was worried Grandpa might figure out I was off my meds.

"What about me? Didn't you think about how what you did might affect me?"

"I'm really sorry. I didn't have much time to think." I sigh. "I'll tell my grandpa we're not spending time together anymore."

"With my luck, he'll think you're lying." He runs his finger around his neck as if his tie is strangling him. Thinking of the mark around Tori's neck, I shiver.

"Back in grade school, Tori and I were best friends." I blow air through pursed lips. "That was obviously a long time ago. So why are you here?" I ask Charlie. I really want to know, but I also want to change the subject. "Were you friends with Tori?"

"You obviously weren't, or you would know not to ask me that. Tori used to call me Pencil, because I'm skinny." He darts a glance at me, and whatever he sees there makes him relent. "My uncle's a homicide detective. That's what I want to be, too. My dad keeps saying engineers or doctors make more money. But being a detective is like solving the world's most interesting puzzles." With one thumb, he points back at the building. "My uncle's checking out who came to the viewing, just like he and the other cops talked to everyone who was at Tori's party. I told him I would come and keep my eyes and ears open." He looks at me and then away. "He thinks I have more friends at school than I really do."

"I've been thinking about Tori a lot since the murder. Trying to figure out who might have done it." I look at Charlie. "So if you were the detective on this case, if you were trying to figure out who killed Tori, what would you do?"

"The first thing is to look at everything about her. It's called victimology." He ticks off a list on his fingers. "Tori's personality, her habits. Her *bad* habits. Her family, her friends, her boyfriend or boyfriends, what kind of student she was. Whether she had some kind of hidden life that put her in danger."

A shiver dances across my skin as I imagine someone pawing through all my secrets. "That's not fair. Why should it be about her? She's the one who was killed. She's the victim! It's like you're saying it's all her fault."

He shrugs, impassive. "The killer *did* choose Tori, not someone else. The cops also need to figure out where she was killed. Was it at her house, Gabriel Park, or someplace else?"

"But Tori left the party. So it can't have been at the house."

He tilts his head, his eyes narrowing. "So someone saw her go?"

"Petra told me she tried to find Tori and couldn't."

"That's not the same thing as being sure she left on her own. Maybe someone killed her and then hid the body in the house or a car until after the party broke up. They'll be looking for signs of a struggle at her house in case she was taken from there or killed there."

"It was a big party, and the house was already pretty trashed when I left. Maybe they won't ever be able to tell." I decide not to mention Tori's dad getting so angry.

Charlie's eyes go wide. "Wait—you were there?"

"Tori invited me."

"No offense, but why? You guys weren't friends."

"We actually *were* friends in grade school. Best friends, in fact. Which is why I want them to catch whoever killed her."

"If she was killed someplace else and then brought to the park, someone would have to carry her body several hundred feet from the parking lot to where it was found. Even though she's not that big, it might be hard to carry her all that way."

I think of how far I had to walk after I left Tori and try to imagine traveling the same distance with her body sagging in my arms. It would be a long trek. "Why would they have buried her in Gabriel Park?"

"It's not like there are a lot of great places to hide a body in our neighborhood. I mean where're you going to put it that it's not going to be found? Bodies are big and they decay. You obviously wouldn't want to put it in your own yard. Put it in a dumpster, and the next homeless guy looking for bottles will find it. Burying it in the wooded part of the park at least upped the chances it might not be found."

And Tori might still be lying there, slowly decomposing, if she hadn't called to me.

I repeat a phrase from the crime shows my grandpa's always watching. "What about motive, means, and opportunity?"

"That's related to victimology. They'll look at who might want Tori dead and why. Who had the opportunity to kill her without being observed. And the means would just be having the gun or the knife or whatever it was that killed her."

Without thinking, I say, "She was strangled."

Charlie's gaze sharpens. "How do you know that?"

Crap. I can't come up with anything better than "That's just what I heard."

THE ULTIMATE PRICE

When I walk into the school auditorium the next afternoon for the funeral, Tori's closed casket has been moved to the left of the stage. An empty podium now stands in the middle. Behind it, Tori's parents and a man with a white collar sit on folding chairs. On the back of the stage, photos flash on a white screen, accompanied by recorded classical music. To the right, our school's choir, dressed in wine-colored robes, waits on risers. Below the stage are three huge floral displays made only of white flowers.

Tori's stretched out on top of her casket, lying on her side. Her head's propped up on one hand. Her top leg rests in front of the bottom one, exaggerating the curve of her hip. She looks like she belongs in some old movie, like she's a sexy lounge singer on top of a grand piano, one who's about to start crooning in a smoky voice.

I can tell by her face that she knows exactly how she looks and that she's chosen her position on purpose. Even if there's only one person in her audience.

She gives me a little waggle of the fingers.

I don't want to, but I smile. I can't help it. Tori's always been over the top, and being dead hasn't changed that at all.

But then in the rows of seats between us I spot Aspen elbowing Petra and pointing at me. They're both looking at me like I'm a sick freak. I turn my head.

The auditorium is already near capacity. Squeezing past a microphone set up in the aisle, I take one of the last seats. Strangers are on either side. On my left is an old man, and on the right is a young mom with a sleeping baby strapped to her chest. I look for Luke and find him in the front row. Detective Geiger and Detective Lauderdale, Charlie's uncle, are scanning the crowd, eyes alert and faces tired. Charlie himself is sitting toward the front but turned so that he can also survey the crowd. When he sees me, he nods. Later this afternoon, after the funeral, he's agreed to compare notes.

On the screen, an infant Tori, dressed in a white dress and a headband bow, lies on her back in a crib. Next a ten-year-old Tori, in helmet and jodhpurs, rides a black horse with four white stockings. That's followed by a preteen Tori in a ballet recital, wearing a costume made mostly of feathers.

"Why did my mom have to use that picture?" Tori rolls her eyes. "I look ridiculous." She sits up. Her bare legs dangle off the edge of the casket. "So what have you learned?"

Under my coat, I'm wearing a black dress topped by a black-and-gray infinity scarf. I chose it because when I dip my chin it covers the lower part of my face. Pressing my hands together as if praying, I drop my head. In a whisper softer than a sigh, I say, "Nothing so far. Not really."

She snorts. "You're a terrible liar, Adele. I can tell you heard something."

I don't want to, but what choice do I have? "Petra said your dad came back early that night. And he was really mad about the party. Could he have—"

"No." Her voice strengthens. "No!"

I make myself whisper the truth. "You were always a little afraid of him."

"But he's my dad." Tori forces a laugh. "My dad."

"Did he ever hurt you?" The headache has slid back into the space behind my right eye, like it never left.

"No." Tori hesitates. "Not really. I mean, he never leaves bruises."

An icy finger traces my spine. "What does that even mean?"

"He's pushed me a few times when I made him mad. Once he grabbed me and wouldn't let me go to a party." She shakes her head decisively. "But he was just watching out for me."

"Okay," I say, although I'm not really letting it drop.

All the seats are taken now. People line up against the walls. Even then there isn't enough space. Out in the hall, people are being directed to the cafeteria, told they will be able to watch the service on TV monitors. For a second, it's tempting to go with them, to just watch the funeral and not be able to see Tori at all.

I stay put.

The choir launches into a hymn, and everyone quiets down. For once there isn't a single false note. Then the pastor comes to the podium. He introduces himself, recites a short prayer, and then starts talking about Tori, enumerating her virtues. I don't see him looking down, but it sounds like he's reading from a piece of paper. And like he never met her.

"Blah, blah, blah," Tori says from her perch on the coffin. Even though the pastor has a microphone, to my ears her voice is much clearer. "How long is he going to go on like that? If I had ever thought about how I wanted my funeral to be—which I never, ever have—it wouldn't have been like this." Her tone is mocking, but her expression betrays her. "I'd rather have a big party."

I don't point out that her last big party didn't turn out so well.

"Look around the room," the pastor commands. "I want you to notice how many people Tori managed to touch in just seventeen years."

At the word *touch*, Tori snorts. "I thought that was my little secret."

The pastor continues to talk about Tori, to remind us how short our lives are, but Tori and I only pay attention to each other.

"Laquanda said that after Luke left, you were dirty dancing with Ethan," I whisper.

"What? No, I wasn't! She's lying." But I hear doubt in her voice.

"That could have made Jazzmin or even Ethan really mad." My fingers rub a circle on my temple, pressing hard, trying to counteract the pain.

"It was a party! That's the kind of thing that happens at parties. So those are your big revelations? Ethan? Jazzmin?" She snorts. "My dad?"

"Have you thought more about Mr. Conner?" I venture, still careful to make only the faintest of sounds.

Tori makes a face. "Drunk or sober, I'd never go anyplace with that creepy guy." She takes a long breath. "But you might be right about why I can't remember what happened that night. It's true I've lost track a few times when I've been drinking. Like someone turned off the lights and everyone moved into a different place and then someone flicks the switch back on again." She snaps her fingers. "It feels like that, even though sometimes a whole night's gone."

"Why didn't you stop drinking, then?"

"It's like walking up to the edge of a railing. Haven't you ever wanted to throw yourself over? You're free, you're falling, you have no control. You can just let go."

Wasn't that what I had wanted that night when I chugged those beers? And look how it turned out. "Until you go splat." The words, which are meant mostly for myself, sound harsh when they come out of my mouth.

Tori's eyes narrow, her expression hardening. "At least I'm living! At least I'm doing things." Her face crumples as she realizes her need to lose control has cost her everything. "I mean, I was." All traces of sassy Tori are gone.

Tori's paid the ultimate price for her mistakes. And it seems unlikely she will ever regain her memories of what happened that night.

"I've been talking to Charlie Lauderdale." When she looks blank, I add, "Pencil."

Her brow furrows. "What would he know?"

"His uncle's one of the detectives working the case."

She tilts her head. "What did he say?"

"That it's important for them to learn all your secrets."

"What?" She crosses her arms. "That's not fair. If they were secret, it's for a good reason."

"But a secret might have gotten you killed. If there's something you think they might not know, tell me."

THE BEATING OF A GIANT HEART

While the choir is singing "Amazing Grace," Tori says, "Okay. You want to know my secrets? I have thought of one person who might have done it. Tom."

Tom? I answer with a raised eyebrow.

"Thomas Hardy."

Mr. Hardy? He's our language arts student teacher. He's always making jokes about his name, saying it all but guaranteed he'd work with words. Thomas Hardy is also the name of an English novelist who died, like, a hundred years ago.

Behind my scarf, I whisper, "But why would Mr. Hardy . . ."

Now it's Tori who answers me with a raised eyebrow. But hers is accompanied by a shrug of one bare shoulder. Understanding dawns. I can't believe either of them could be so stupid. "You were seeing him? What about Luke?"

The old man next to me glances over, and I realize I put a little too much force behind my whisper. I fake cough like I need to clear my throat.

"Tom's not my boyfriend or anything. He's just fun."

"And you're a minor." My whisper is lighter than a sigh. "He could get—have gotten—in so much trouble!" No wonder he's looked haggard all week.

Tori crosses her arms. "That's why I've been thinking about him. You need to check him out. He wasn't here yesterday, and he's not here today. To be honest, I'm insulted."

"You broke up with Luke just because *I* kissed *him*." Tori seems to be implying she did much more with Mr. Hardy—and that it was her idea.

"But we would have gotten back together. We always get back together. Luke and me, we're not that different. He understands me."

Could Mr. Hardy really have done it? I imagine how it might have played out. After Tori found me with Luke and then kicked us both out, her ego must have been bruised. According to Petra, she starting drinking even harder, acting like she was having a good time. According to Ms. Borka, the alcohol could have made stupid ideas seem like good ones. Without leaving any memories behind.

Maybe Tori called Mr. Hardy and he came over. Not to comfort her, as she had asked, but to tell her she had to shut up about them. To tell her she was risking everything. Not for her, but for him. If people found out, he'd definitely lose his job. And he'd never be able to be a teacher again. He might even go to prison.

I imagine Tori protesting, starting to cause a scene. And Mr. Hardy panicking.

I've seen him get into his car in the school parking lot. The first thing he does is take off the lanyard with his name tag and hang it from his rearview mirror. Could he have strangled her with the lanyard's cloth cord? I imagine him looping it around Tori's neck and pulling back. Her fingers clawing at her throat. His determined expression.

While I'm thinking, Mr. Rasmussen takes his turn at the microphone. "My daughter was an amazing girl," he says. "She was strong and smart and sometimes sassy."

"Sometimes," Tori's echo starts out mocking, but then breaks. She puts her hands over her face. Her shoulders shake as she begins to cry. My headache has grown to the point that I have to close one eye.

"My daughter was a force to be reckoned with," Mr. Rasmussen continues. "And as for the person who killed her"—he pounds his fist on the podium—"I guarantee that person will be reckoning with that force"—*pound*—"not only for the remainder of their pathetic life"—*pound*—"but for the rest of eternity as they burn in hell." My headache pulses in time with each blow, which is like the beating of a giant heart.

If Tori's father is really the killer, how can he be so passionate? Or are his anger and tears fueled by guilt?

The auditorium smells close and faintly sweaty. All

that air being pulled in and pushed out of hundreds of lungs, losing its oxygen.

Mrs. Rasmussen is able to say even less, the words gasped out between sobs. "If I . . . could have . . . Tori . . . back with me for . . . even one more day . . ."

"Mom—" Tori gets off her coffin, then stretches out her hand, trying desperately to reach her mother. But even at the end of the tether there's still at least five feet between them. Tori's face is contorted, mouth stretched wide, eyes squinted, but there are no tears.

After her parents finish speaking, the pastor invites the audience to share memories of Tori at one of the mics set up throughout the auditorium. While he speaks, Tori wipes her dry eyes, composing herself.

Aspen goes first. "I will miss talking to Tori so much. No one can take her place." She starts to sob.

"Good Lord." Tori shakes her head. "It's not like we were even that close. That's Aspen for you. She loves the drama."

A laugh spurts out of my mouth. Under my scarf, I press my lips together. Try to contort my face into sadness.

But Aspen's head whipped in my direction. Now she stares at me with narrowed eyes. I know she's not fooled.

One by one, people go up to the mics. Teachers, neighbors, parents, and lots of kids from our school. People talk about how funny Tori was, how pretty, how smart. Charlie watches all of them. I can tell he's making mental notes, maybe looking for discrepancies. But who's going to say something bad about Tori in front of all these people?

What would people say about me if I died?

Adele was quiet and a little weird. She saw things and then she had to take drugs so she wouldn't. The first time she kissed a guy, she was drunk and he was someone else's boyfriend. Oh, and once she tried to fake kiss some guy but accidentally kissed him for real for a second. She lived with her grandfather. She didn't have any close friends. She never caused any trouble.

Suddenly, the way Tori lived her life seems a lot more appealing. She may have acted recklessly, she may have hurt people's feelings, but at least she lived.

When it's Petra's turn at the mic, her voice is shaking. "All I have to say is you took a beautiful soul from this earth. How can you live with yourself? Tori was only seventeen years old. She didn't deserve this."

Tori rolls her eyes. "But it would be okay if I were thirty-seven? Ninety-seven?"

I have to admit, I like this Tori much better. This version is honest, sarcastic, and funny, but now I can also see her vulnerability.

In the row ahead of me, Maddy P and Maddy D start to wail, their arms around each other.

"Everybody's sorry," Tori observes, "but it's like they're sorry for themselves. Not for me."

In a strangled voice, Murphy says, "I will never forget how Tori's face looked when she was laughing. Her laugh made you laugh."

At his words, a bit of the tension goes out of the room. A few people smile and nod.

I'm so lost in my thoughts I don't see Luke going up to a mic. The sound of his voice makes me raise my head.

"I've been trying to think about what to say about Tori. But the problem is, I can't really believe she's dead. Because if there's one thing Tori was, it was alive." His voice cracks. "She was one hundred percent alive."

Tori puts her hands over her face. Speaking through her fingers, she says, "You have to tell Luke I'm still here."

"How can I?" I whisper. "He won't believe it."

"We could talk through you."

Even if Luke believed me, how long would such one-way conversations be satisfying?

After a few more people speak, the pastor begins to wrap things up. "Tori's death reminds us that you don't know what's going to happen tomorrow. So don't leave words unsaid. Tell your friends and family you love them." He looks out over the crowd. "Now go in peace."

Next to me, the baby starts to fuss as people get to their feet and shuffle out to the aisle. Deciding to wait a few minutes, I bow my head like I'm praying. I ignore the people who push past me, stepping on my feet.

"Tori, I have to go soon," I whisper.

"But . . . but I'll see you again, right? You'll come visit me at the cemetery."

I realize it's my choice. This could be the last time I see Tori. The idea has a lot of appeal. What do I really owe her? Even if I do find her killer, it won't fix anything. It won't bring her back to life.

And if being close to one dead person makes me feel this bad, what will hundreds do?

"Adele?" Tori says.

"Adele?" a man's voice says.

It's Detective Geiger. He's standing in the aisle, looking at me with his tired blue eyes.

"There are a few things I need to clear up from our interview the other day. Would it be possible to talk to you?"

YOU HAVE TO HELP ME

"Would you mind if we went down to the station?" Detective Geiger asks. "That's where my notes are."

My mind is racing but not going anyplace. It's like pushing the accelerator on Grandpa's truck while it's still in Park.

"What does he want?" Tori demands from the stage.

"You're not in custody," Geiger says when the silence stretches out. "We just need your help to clear up a few inconsistencies."

"Sure, I guess that's okay." I don't want to go with him, but I can't figure out a good way to say no.

We head to the exit, the detective's hand under my elbow. Heads turn. Eyes narrow. Charlie stares at us, his mouth half open.

"Adele, where are you going? Adele!" Tori's shout is

like a punch to the side of my head. But there's no way I can answer her without Geiger noticing, so I don't.

It's a relief to step out in the rain-scented air. My headache immediately starts to recede.

"My car's right over there." Geiger points his chin at a dark blue four-door sedan parked not far from a shiny black hearse.

In the car, he turns on a news station. On the drive there, we listen to stories about a bombing in Turkey and a snowstorm in Colorado. He parks in an underground lot filled mostly with marked police cars. In the elevator, he waves a card key over a sensor before pushing the button for the eighth floor. I can't think of any small talk, and it seems safer to stay quiet anyway.

After the elevator door opens, I follow the detective as he walks past a warren of cubicles. There are more men than women, more plain clothes than uniforms. They take no notice of us. They're busy talking on phones or to each other, looking at screens, typing on keyboards. The only thing that keeps it from looking like any other busy office is a photo lying on someone's desk. Eight by ten, it's a color close-up of a knife wound.

Geiger grabs a gray file, a tape recorder, and a slim black folder off one of the desks we pass, then opens a door and waves me inside. It's as basic as a room can be. Three chairs that don't match, a small table, a gray speckled linoleum floor, and nothing on the walls.

"I'm going to record this just like I did when we spoke on Tuesday. Okay?"

"Sure." I take one of the chairs as he sets the recorder on the table between us.

"Today is December first, and this is Detective Geiger talking with Adele Meeker." He looks at me. "Adele, this is just a casual conversation. I want to clarify a few things, and we'll be out of here as quickly as possible. We appreciate you being willing to help us out."

"Okay." I remind myself to say the bare minimum.

He pulls out his notebook. "Don't worry if you feel you have already answered these questions. What time did you arrive at Tori's house for the party?"

"Around eight."

Geiger takes me over the evening minute by minute, step by step. Had I used any drugs? How much beer had I had to drink? Who had I seen there? What had they been doing? Who had they been with? Who had I talked to? What about?

He's scribbling in his notebook when something starts to rise from the linoleum floor behind him.

I suck in my breath.

His head jerks up. He looks at me, then behind him, then at me again. "Is everything okay, Adele?"

So whatever the dark, round thing is, he can't see it. A needle of pain slips behind my right eye.

"Um, it's fine." I try to pick up the thread of what I was saying. "So Murphy and Justin were play fighting, and . . ."

The thing behind him keeps rising, without distorting the linoleum, like the floor is a still pool of water. Then it tilts, and I realize it's a woman's head.

What's happening? All I know is I'd better act as if nothing is wrong. "And Justin and Murphy were talking about the best way to hit someone. You know, in a fight." I resolutely focus on Geiger, not on the dark-haired young woman. Her head is all the way through the floor now, as well as her neck and the tops of her bare shoulders.

She's staring straight at me.

"Oh my God." Her voice is rusty. "You can see me."

No. Not another dead person. Tori is bad enough. This woman's face is gaunt, her teeth yellow. Despite that, I don't think she's much older than me. Or at least, that's how old she was when she died. Now she's stuck being nineteen or so forever, just like Tori's going to be wearing that halter dress for eternity.

I tear my gaze away and paste it back on Geiger. Who is staring straight at me.

"You have to help me," the woman says from behind him.

That's what everyone wants from me these days. I rub at the now familiar pain in my temple.

"Adele," Geiger says, "you seem really wound up, like there's something you're not telling me."

I'm being pulled in two directions, between the living and the dead. And neither of them is happy with me.

"I'm telling you everything," I lie. "It's just that I have a headache."

"Please—" The woman's voice breaks. "After all these years, you have to help me. Please. My name's Lisa. Lisa McMasters. You have to tell Mark my name."

Mark must be Detective Geiger. But that doesn't

matter. Because I'm not going to do what she asks. I'm in enough trouble as it is.

Geiger resumes his questioning. "And you said this was just before the game of hide-and-seek got started? What time was that?"

"Maybe around nine?"

Lisa's voice is like a drill in my head. "Why won't you listen to me? I know you can hear me. I know you can see me."

I cup my hand around my eye, so it partly blocks her from my peripheral vision.

Geiger sighs. "You won't even meet my eyes, Adele. What is it you're not telling me?"

What am I going to say? That looking directly at him means looking at the dead woman behind him?

"You have to tell him who I am and who killed me," Lisa insists.

Like someone making a snarky comment, I cough words into my fist. "I can't." The fake cough is followed by a real cough.

Geiger gets to his feet. "Do you need something to drink, Adele? I can get you a soda or water from the vending machine."

Do I want him to leave me alone with nothing but a dead girl for company? But maybe I'll be able to explain to her that I can't afford to be seen talking to someone other people can't see.

"Actually, water would be great. Thank you." I've seen enough cop shows to know that even after he leaves, someone is probably still watching me on a camera.

Listening to me. Waiting for me to mutter a confession to myself. Or to fall asleep with my head on the table, proof that I'm an uncaring killer.

I pull my scarf over my mouth, prop one elbow on the table, press my hands together, and tilt my head over them. I can always claim to have been praying. Praying with my eyes open, focused on a section of the floor that to anyone else will appear empty.

"Don't pretend like you can't see me. I know you can," Lisa says. "But why?"

My answer is the ghost of a whisper. "All I know is it runs in my family. Why are you here?" I think of Rebecca at the museum. "Are you buried under the building or something?"

"No. My skull's in a box in the evidence room. It's the next floor down."

"That explains why I can only see your head."

"What? No, I'm all me. I'm all here." Lisa grits her teeth and then slowly, a pale, slender hand pushes its way up through the linoleum. The fingers wave at me before the hand slides back out of sight.

How can I see all of Lisa if only her skull is in the evidence room? Then I remember that those misty ropes always run from the back of the head. And it's the skull that holds the brain, which in turn holds our thoughts, our memories, the things that make us *us*. It must be enough.

Lisa speaks into my silence. "I've been here for years. These days, I mostly just sleep. But then I woke up because

I felt you somehow. I had to climb up the shelves to get here. This is as far as I can go."

"Are there other dead people there?"

"A couple of times there have been. But then their bones get identified and taken away. Mostly I'm alone." Her voice sounds so weary. "That's why you have to tell him my name. So I can go too."

"How many years have you been there?"

She sighs. "I've lost track. I was murdered in 1977 and dumped in the woods. And then there were"—she makes a face—"animals. A couple of years later, some hunters found my skull and called the police. But they didn't find the rest of me, and they couldn't tell who I was. So they put my skull in a box and stuck it in the evidence room. I've been there ever since. I just want my family to know where I am so they can take me home to North Carolina. And at least if I was in a cemetery I wouldn't be alone. My parents must be gone now too. I'm hoping I'll be buried next to them."

"You were murdered?"

"I worked at a truck stop. One of my customers killed me."

"You were a waitress?"

Lisa looks away. "Not exactly."

I get it. "Oh."

"The guy who did it was one of my regulars. His name was Johnny. Johnny O'Reilly. Balding guy with these pale blue eyes the color of ice."

"Look, Lisa," I whisper, "there's no way I could tell

the police and have them believe me. They'll just think I'm—" The door opens with a creak. I press my lips together.

Geiger's got two bottles of water, and he sets both of them in front of me.

He sits, and for a long time he's quiet. I'm careful not to look at either him or Lisa. Instead I study the blue plastic water bottle as if I've never seen one before.

Finally he sighs. "Adele, you know you're not under arrest, not even in trouble. We're just talking here, and you can leave anytime you want. But at the same time, this thing is going forward, and we need your help." He slips a photo out of the gray file and puts it next to the water. "We have to talk about this, Adele. And this time, I need you to tell me the truth."

The photo's black-and-white and blurry. It shows a person wearing a hoodie, talking on a pay phone mounted on a brick wall.

It could be anyone.

But it's me.

WHICH THINGS ARE REAL

Judging by the angle, there must be a camera mounted above the entrance to the 7-Eleven. Should I claim the person in the photo isn't me? But if they fingerprinted the phone, all they would need to do is take my prints. Why didn't I wipe it clean before I left?

Geiger stabs the photo with a thick finger. "Adele, we know this is you. We know you're the one who called 9-1-1 to report Tori's body. So how did you know it was buried in Gabriel Park?"

"Let me guess," Lisa interjects. "She told you."

I keep my focus on the detective. Like picking my way across a barely iced-over pond, I try to mostly tell the truth without falling through.

"I was cutting through the park, and I noticed . . ." I almost say *her dress*, but at the last second I realize the real dress was buried. "Under one of the trees, the dirt was a different color and mounded up. From the shape, I wondered if it was a grave. But I didn't really believe it, not until I brushed the dirt off Tori's face."

"I'll bet she didn't believe it either," Lisa says. "When I was out in the woods, it took me forever to accept that I was dead." It takes effort to pretend I don't see Lisa, don't hear her. I worry the headache is making me forget to hide any reaction to her.

Geiger is silent for a long moment. Finally he says, "Not many girls would be brave enough to get down on their knees and actually start to dig up a grave."

"Maybe it was more just being stupid." I close my eyes for a second, remembering the horror both Tori and I had felt when we saw her dead face. "And then when I realized it was her, I went across the street and called 9-1-1."

"Why didn't you call from your cell phone?"

My thoughts skitter. Isn't that what an innocent person would have done? "It was super low on battery. I was afraid it would cut out in the middle."

Geiger's blue eyes bore into me. "And why didn't you give your name to the dispatcher?"

"I wanted to help. But I didn't want to get *too* involved." I realize this doesn't quite jibe with my earlier explanation about a low battery.

"But you are involved now, Adele. You're in this thing up to your neck. For one thing, you disturbed a crime scene."

"It's not looking good for you," Lisa chimes in.

I ignore her, as well as the pain in my head. "I'm sorry. I didn't know what it was when I started."

"We have casts of the shoe prints we found at the scene, but it seems likely that you walked all over the killer's prints, replacing them with your own. Do you still have the shoes you wore that day?"

I hadn't even thought of that. What if I screwed up the best chance the cops have of catching the killer? "Yeah, they're at home."

"What brand are they?"

"Vans. Black slip-ons."

"We'll need to check them. Just to cover all the bases, I'd like to take prints of the bottom of the shoes you're wearing now." He opens up the slim black folder and removes some loose forms.

"But I wasn't wearing these shoes that night. I'm sure of it."

Shrugging, he flips back a black rubbery sheet from a yellow pad on one side of the folder, then lays one of the forms, blank side up, on the other side and sets the whole thing on the floor. "It's just for exclusionary purposes."

It's clear there's no point in arguing. I stand up and follow his instructions to step on the yellow pad and then the paper, leaving a footprint. Then I do the same thing with my other foot.

He puts my shoe prints in the file folder. "Now I want you to think carefully before you answer. Did you take anything from the scene? A note, a piece of clothing, even a gum wrapper?"

"No." It's a relief to be back in a space where I don't have to lie.

"The medical examiner is releasing the results today. Tori was strangled. I want you to think back. When you were near the grave or leaving the park, did you see anything that could have been used to strangle her? Like a cord or a dog leash?"

A leash. I hadn't even thought of that. When we were kids, the Rasmussens didn't own a dog, and I hadn't seen any signs of one at the party. Tori's body wasn't far from the park's popular off-leash area, but the chance that a late-night dog walker was also a murderer seems slim.

Geiger switches tacks. "I had an interesting conversation while I was getting your water. Are you under a doctor's care, Adele?"

"He wants to know if you're crazy," Lisa says helpfully.

"I'm a patient of Dr. Duncan's."

Geiger nods. "And what kind of doctor is Dr. Duncan?"

"He's a psychiatrist."

"And what's your diagnosis?"

"Schizophrenia." No point in telling him I think it's wrong, but I also don't want him thinking I'm like Dr. Jekyll and Mr. Hyde, that there could be an evil Adele as well as the one he's seeing now. "A lot of people think that means you have a split personality, but that's wrong."

"No, schizophrenia means having trouble telling which things are real." Geiger leans closer. "Do you have that trouble, Adele?"

"No." I don't sound convincing. Of course, seeing the head of a long-dead girl poking through the floor of a police interrogation room doesn't help.

"But maybe you had some trouble the night of the party," Geiger says. "Maybe you got confused and something happened that you never meant to have happen. It's understandable, really."

I don't say anything, but Lisa does. "I think he's fishing. He's hoping you'll fill in the blanks. I've seen him do this a hundred times. He can even lie to you. It's legal."

"I didn't do anything to Tori." I want to sound certain, but my voice trembles as I think about blackouts.

He crosses his arms. "But maybe you know who did."

"I don't!" I rub my temple. The throbbing is making it hard to think.

"Let me be honest, Adele. You're in a hole. We already know what happened, and this thing is going to wrap up soon. If you'll just tell us what really happened, we'll type it up, and that will be that. Then we can all go home."

"I already told you what happened. There's nothing more to tell."

"I'm not here to judge you." Geiger uncrosses his arms and rests his hands on his knees. "But I can tell you're scared. What are you scared of, Adele?"

"I'm not scared." But my voice shakes. "I just have a headache."

"You're scared," he repeats. When I don't answer, he says, "Adele, look at me."

I do. Reluctantly. The pouches under his eyes look like bruises. I keep my focus tight, ignoring Lisa.

"You're scared because you know the truth. We know you were involved. I listen to people day and night, and I recognize deception when I hear it. Tell me the truth. What happened that night?"

"I already told you the truth. I went to Tori's party, we got in a fight, and I went home and went to bed. And that's it. I didn't hurt her."

From the folder, he takes another photo. This one is a candid snapshot of Tori, in color. "It's all over for Tori. And for what?" He slides it next to the black-and-white photo of me. In her photo, she's sunny and smiling, while I'm furtive and lurking in mine.

"Mark's a good cop, and he thinks you did it, that you killed this Tori girl," Lisa says. "Did you?"

I want to scream. I'm barely holding it together as it is, without a long-dead girl who insists on commenting on everything and asking me questions I can't answer.

"I'm sorry. I can't help you. I would if I could, but I didn't do it, and I don't know who did."

Geiger sighs. "Do you always wear that necklace?"

My hand goes to the thick leather cord. "Yeah."

"Do you mind if I take it?"

"Wh-what? Why?" I stutter. And then I know why.

Because he thinks I used it to kill Tori.

From his file folder, Geiger takes a small manila envelope labeled EVIDENCE in black block letters. He holds the edges between his fingers so it pouches open. "Can you drop it in?"

Slowly, I pull the cord over my head. Is it possible I did this a week ago? That I got blackout drunk, slipped my own necklace off, dropped it over Tori's neck, and then yanked back?

No. No, it can't be.

I ball up the long cord and then let it fall into the envelope. The only time I don't wear the necklace is when I shower. Is that why I suddenly feel so naked?

WHAT HAVE YOU GONE
AND DONE?

We're back in Detective Geiger's car, and the radio is still talking about the blizzard in Colorado. But everything feels different. Now I know I'm a suspect. And he knows—or at least he thinks he does—that I'm mentally ill.

My hand keeps going to the empty spot where my locket should be. Geiger even confiscated my phone, after asking me if he could. There really didn't seem any way I could say no.

I feel wrung out, hollow. As I was leaving the interview room, Lisa broke down crying, begging me to find a way to get her out of the evidence room, saying that even being in the woods had been better.

Geiger said he could give me a ride back to wherever I wanted. When I said I wanted to go home, he didn't even ask for my address.

As soon as we turn in to the parking lot, I know why. In the visitors' spaces, a black-and-white police car is parked next to a sedan that looks identical to the one we're in. And in the back of the lot, an old blue pickup is being slowly winched onto a flatbed tow truck. A uniformed cop is shining her flashlight on the ground where it was.

"That's my grandpa's truck!" My stomach drops.

"Yup," Geiger agrees, and I realize he already knows. He pulls up to the curb in front of my apartment.

"What are you going to do with it?" The truck is Grandpa's baby. He taught me to drive in it, but even after I got my license last year, he's never let me drive it by myself.

"We're just following the leads where they take us, Adele." He's watching me carefully, gauging my reaction.

"But that's how my grandpa gets to work."

"We're taking it to a secure facility so we can search it. Depending on what we find, we'll either retain it or release it." Geiger tilts his head, his eyes narrowing. "Tell me, has Tori ever been in it?"

For a second, my thoughts stutter as I think about blackouts. "No," I say. "Never." Hoping it's the right answer.

"We'll be in touch. Do you still have my phone number?" When I nod numbly, he says, "Call me anytime, day or night, if there's something you want to tell me."

I get out of the car and look up the stairs. Out of our already open door comes a cop wearing latex gloves. In his arms are two bankers' boxes, stacked one on top of the other. Behind the cop is Charlie's uncle. Detective Lauderdale is also carrying two bankers' boxes, only on top of his is my laptop computer. Both of them look down at me with thousand-yard stares. Not friendly, not even unfriendly. Like they're just doing what has to be done and nothing will deter them.

After they pass me without speaking, I run up the stairs.

Grandpa is sitting on the couch with his head in his hands. Around him are heaps of belongings pulled from closets and shelves and then piled on the floor.

Without saying anything, I walk past him and into my room. The sheets and blankets have been stripped off the bed and then left in a tangle on the bare mattress. My dresser drawers gape open, clearly pawed through. The only shoes in the room are the ones I'm wearing.

My closet holds a dozen empty hangers. It takes me a minute to figure out what the missing clothes have in common.

They all have a drawstring.

Feeling like my head is a balloon and my feet are far away, I walk back out into the living room. "Did they have a warrant?"

He nods.

Not knowing what else to do, I start cleaning up. Grandpa doesn't do anything. He doesn't get up, he doesn't help, he doesn't even look at me. He just sits with his head hanging, looking every year of his age.

With everything out of place, I can see how bad my dusting has been, only hitting the easily accessible surfaces. I go into the kitchen. It isn't as bad as the other rooms, although drawers and cabinets gape open. I wad up some paper towels, wet them, and go back out to the living room to wipe away the dust.

As I work in silence, I try to remember what I've googled on my computer and/or phone and how it might look when the cops examine my search history. I've used search terms like "strangle" and "ligature," but all of them were after Tori was dead.

When Grandpa finally speaks, I jump.

"What have you gone and done, Adele?"

"The cops are acting like I might have killed Tori. Which is ridiculous." I force a laugh, but his sad expression doesn't change. "You know I didn't do it." My voice sounds too high. "Right?"

I wait.

He doesn't answer.

With every second that passes, it feels like there's a vacuum in my chest where my heart should be. Like I'm going to implode. Tears flood my eyes.

"Come on, Grandpa, you know me."

He finally lifts his head. His eyes are red-rimmed. "I do know you. And I love you. I love you so much, Adele. I also knew Tori. I saw how she treated you."

Stunned, I slump on the couch next to him. He thinks I did it. And then he says something that makes things even worse.

"I looked in the bathroom, Adele. I filled your prescription three weeks ago. You should only have seven left. But the bottle is nearly full."

SATURDAY, DECEMBER 1, 4:41 P.M.

TRYING TO FILL
IN THE BLANKS

Grandpa covers his face with his twisted hands.
My stomach bottoms out. He thinks I'm a killer.
And he knows about the pills.

"Okay, I did stop taking them," I admit. "But I didn't
kill Tori."

"That detective told me you're the one who found her
body." Dropping his hands, he raises his rheumy eyes to
me. "Is that because you're the one who left her there in
the first place?"

"No! The reason I knew she was there was
because—because she called to me when I was cutting
through the park on Monday." It's a relief to let go and
speak the truth. "And once I realized she was dead, I
called 9-1-1."

His face goes still and sad. "So you think she was

talking to you." It's not really a question. "*After* she was dead."

"It was like that girl in the museum, the one I thought was an actor, the one who really died on the Oregon Trail."

He scrubs his face with his hands. "And when did you stop taking your medication?"

"A couple of weeks ago, I missed one by accident." I try to make him understand. "Then the next morning, it was like the world was in color again, when it had been black-and-white forever. When I'm on the pills, I'm really only half alive. Do you have any idea how bad they make me feel?"

Grandpa gets to his feet and raises one gnarled hand. Before I even realize what's happening, he slaps me.

My mouth falls open as the blood rushes to my stinging skin. The slap wasn't particularly hard. It's just the shock of it. My grandpa has never hit me. Never. Not even raised his hand.

Tears sparkle in his eyes. "And do you have any idea what happens when you're *not* on them, Adele? You get like your mom, your grandma, your great-grandma. You see things that aren't there! You talk to people that don't exist."

"It's not that they don't exist. It's that they're dead."

He's breathing hard. "Your mom must have put those thoughts into your head. Did she tell you the whole story, Adele? It's familial schizophrenia. That means it's in your blood. In your genes. Miriam's mom, your great-grandmother, was convinced she was possessed by Satan. At funerals, she said she could hear the spirits of the dead calling out to her. Your grandma and I, we knew that was just superstition. We tried to persuade her to get help, but she killed herself."

I stare at him, shocked into silence.

"And then things got so much worse. Because at her own mother's funeral, it was Miriam claiming she could still see her mom. Even talk to her. She tried to tell me that her mother wasn't dead, at least not all the way. I took her to a psychiatrist. He said part of her brain was sick and needed to be dealt with, just like cutting mold off a piece of cheese. So he gave Miriam a lobotomy. Your mom was only a few months old."

Grandpa has just said more words than I normally hear him speak in a week. How desperate had he been, that he let someone destroy part of his wife's brain?

"Did it work?" I only have one memory of my grandma, from when I was five or six. I waited with my mom in a parking lot, waited for my grandma's head to appear in the fourth-floor window of a big gray building. And my grandpa was standing next to her, raising her limp hand and calling to me and my mom to wave back.

"Did it work?" Grandpa echoes. He blinks, and a tear rolls down his face. "Well, Miriam didn't see ghosts anymore." He makes a sound like a laugh. "She also didn't remember her own name, let alone mine. She was more like a ghost herself. The nurses let her have this empty coffeepot, and she would sit in her room, endlessly pouring imaginary coffee from that empty pot." His voice shakes.

All the time he's been speaking, I've been combing through my memories of my mom. Before the car accident that took her life, she had been acting strangely. Sometimes she even left me at home alone in the middle of the night. And when she returned from wherever she had been, her eyes were wide and lost.

"What really happened to my mom?" He had been the one who broke the news that she was dead. That was the last time I saw him cry.

"Your mom had it so hard after your dad died. She tried to keep it together for you. But she was seduced by the idea that he was really still alive. Just like you must want Tori to still be alive. Your mom began spending more and more time at your dad's grave. Talking and laughing like someone was there and speaking back to her. Eventually, she lost her job. She didn't care about the living anymore. She had a child—a child!—and she let herself get lost in this sick fantasy."

His words are coming slower. "The day that she died, I went to the cemetery and told her she had to come home. That she had to be a mother to you. I forced her into the car. But when I stopped at a light, she jumped out and started running back. She ran right in front of a truck."

Sorrow weights my bones. It's hard for me to even speak. "Have you ever thought that what we've all said might be true? That we really can see the dead if we're where their bones are?"

"Listen to yourself, Adele. It's just your mind telling you a story. Something bad happened between you and Tori, and rather than admitting it, you made yourself believe that she's not really dead. Just like Miriam found a way to make her mom alive again. Just like your mother wouldn't admit Ben was gone." His face contorts. "I love you no matter what. But now I'm going to lose you. Just like I've lost everyone else."

What's Grandpa going to do? Is he going to kick me out? Is he going to force me to be hospitalized?

"I told the police about our family," he says. "Because it's the only thing that might save you. You won't go to prison for killing Tori. Not with our family history. No, you'll end up in a mental hospital, probably for the rest of your life." He puts his hands over his face, and his thin shoulders hunch as he starts to sob.

SATURDAY, DECEMBER 1, 5:13 P.M.

DO YOU REALLY WANT TO KNOW THE TRUTH?

'm locked in the bathroom, mostly because I can't stand to see my grandpa cry. My mind is whirling, and my thoughts can't find purchase. The eyes that meet mine in the mirror are red and watery. I guess that's what happens when you spend most of the day talking to dead people and then learn that the person you love most in the whole world believes you're a killer.

And that the cops do, too.

Is there any chance they're right?

Tori wants me to find her murderer. But what if it *is* me? Ms. Borka said getting blackout drunk makes you act on impulses that the sober you would know were wrong. What if Tori caught up to me after she left the party? It's easy to imagine her mocking me, telling me there was no way someone as great as Luke would be into me.

Would that be enough to make me snap, to decide to shut her up?

"No," I say to the girl in the mirror. "No."

I feel as stuck as Tori or Lisa, and as powerless to change things. Even if I'm innocent, does it matter? I imagine a jury listening to the circumstantial evidence. I had the motive, the means, and even the opportunity to kill Tori.

The police think I did it. My own grandpa thinks I did it. There's only one person who can save me.

And that's me.

But to do it, I'm going to need help. From the same guy who had already agreed to help me.

Back in my room, I find the laundry bag that was emptied out on the carpet and fill it again. I add the contents of my underwear drawer, which was pawed through by strange hands.

"I'm going to do laundry," I tell Grandpa. Sitting slumped on the couch, he just nods.

After I start my wash, I knock on the door of Charlie's apartment. When he answers, he's still dressed in funeral clothes, that too-big suit that must belong to his dad. Still, it makes him look older. I can almost imagine him being the detective he wants to be.

"I need to talk to you," I say.

He keeps his hand on the knob and doesn't open the door any wider. "What about?"

"Tori's murder."

"I don't think we should talk anymore, Adele. My uncle was just searching your apartment. It seems you're the prime suspect." His mouth twists. "And last night someone told me what happened at the party, how you kissed Luke and then Tori kicked you out. None of this looks good."

"All that's true, but I didn't kill Tori." My voice cracks. "Please—can I come in?"

After a moment, he opens the door wider. Taking two quick steps ahead of me, he sweeps a sleeping bag and pillow off a battered navy blue couch and into a closet. All the units on the ground floor are one-bedrooms. I wonder whether it's Charlie or his dad who's stuck with the couch. I'm betting Charlie.

"Where's your dad?" I haven't met him yet, but a couple of times I've seen a guy in the parking lot who must be him. He's tall and brown-eyed like Charlie and Detective Lauderdale, but not nearly as skinny as either.

"At our old house." Charlie rolls his eyes. "Trying to sweet-talk my stepmom into taking him back. The house is in her name, and she makes a lot more money than my dad. So cheating on her was a pretty stupid thing to do. Not to mention not very nice." He exhales forcefully. "But he never thinks with his head."

I'm not sure what to say in response, so I settle for a simple "I'm sorry."

He sits on one end of the couch, so I take the other. There's four feet between us. It's kind of a weird arrangement, but there isn't anyplace else to sit except two mismatched chairs in the dining nook. And it would be weirder if I'd sat in the middle.

"My uncle told me they released the autopsy results today. And it was like you said. Tori was strangled."

"Not with hands." I touch my neck. "With something narrow around her throat."

Charlie's eyes narrow. "How do you know it was a ligature?"

"Because I'm the one who found her body. I saw the mark."

He puts his hands over his face. From behind them, he says, "Just stop, Adele. Stop talking and get yourself a lawyer."

"What do you mean?"

He runs his hands through his hair, tugging on it. "Because it seems pretty likely that you're guilty. And I'm going to tell my uncle anything you say."

"The cops already know I found the body. But I didn't kill Tori. I don't know how I can prove that to them or you or anyone, but I didn't." The words are as much for myself as for him. "Besides, won't there be evidence that shows I'm not the one who did it?"

His expression becomes thoughtful. "Well, that ligature furrow around Tori's throat is going to tell the police a lot. An electrical cord leaves a different mark than a metal chain or a shoelace or a clothesline or a belt. And some people bring a ligature with them and others just improvise. If they can figure out what the ligature was, then it might tell them who did it. They might even be able to get fibers from it. How wide was it? Did it break the skin?"

Closing my eyes, I try to remember. "It was pretty

thin. I think thinner than a pencil. And it looked like it made a groove in her skin but didn't cut it." I open my eyes and take a deep breath. "Detective Geiger took my locket. It's on a thick black cord."

"They'll check it for Tori's DNA."

"And they won't find any," I say, hoping I'm right. "Everywhere I go, I see things that could have killed Tori. Electrical cords, the cords on blinds, lanyards, dog leashes . . . I heard that after I left the party, Tori started dirty dancing with Ethan. And that made Jazzmin really mad. Maybe Ethan wanted more and Tori wouldn't give it to him. He wears that survival bracelet made out of paracord. And Jazzmin always has on one of those cloth headbands. Either one of those could have been the murder weapon."

"Except Ethan sits in front of me in math, and he's still wearing that stupid survival bracelet. And a headband—it would probably just stretch. I could totally see Jazzmin sulking, but sulking doesn't lead to murder."

"Okay, what about Tori's creepy neighbor? Mr. Conner? That old guy who always wears a bolo tie? He tried to give me a ride home after I left the party, and he didn't want to take no for an answer. And Tori told me he liked to spy on her when she was sunbathing."

"She did?" Charlie tilts his head. "I didn't think you guys had been friends since back in grade school."

"She just mentioned it."

"Well, Mr. Conner makes a lot more sense than Ethan or Jazzmin. Did you tell Detective Geiger about him trying to give you a ride?"

"Yeah."

"Then I'm sure they're looking at him."

"And there's her dad. He came home a day early, and I heard he got really mad when he realized she was throwing a party. Maybe he snapped."

"Maybe," Charlie echoes dubiously.

"There's one other person I was thinking might have done it. Tori was spending time with Tom Hardy. The student teacher."

Charlie's head jerks back. "What do you mean, spending time?"

For an answer, I press my lips together and raise my eyebrows, echoing Tori's coyness.

Charlie shakes his head. "Yeah, right. I don't think so. No teacher would be that stupid."

"But she told me."

He sighs in exasperation. "I don't understand you, Adele. You keep acting like you have the inside scoop on Tori, but you weren't her friend. At least not for years. When did she tell you all this stuff?"

It feels like I've climbed up on the edge of a bridge and am looking into the iron-gray water far below. "Do you really want to know the truth, Charlie? Because there's no way you'll believe me."

SATURDAY, DECEMBER 1, 5:28 P.M.

PROVE THAT I'M NOT

"Try me, Adele." Charlie looks me in the eye.

After taking a deep breath, I jump in. "I can see the dead. Even talk to them. It's why I know things about Tori that only a friend would know. Because she talked to me after I found her body."

Charlie's lips twitch as if he wants to ask a question. Or maybe laugh in sickened disbelief. Instead, he keeps quiet.

"I've been like this my whole life. It runs in my family."

He raises an eyebrow. "So you can see ghosts?"

"I don't know what they are. I can only see them if I'm near their bones. And they can't go places where their bones aren't. So it's not like a haunting; it's not like those stories when the spirit lingers where something bad happened. Not unless their bones happen to be buried there." Thinking of Lisa, I add, "Or even just their skull."

"And you were able to see Tori? Like she was alive?" Each word is spaced farther from the next and filled with more doubt.

I nod. "And talk to her."

"If she could talk to you, why couldn't she tell you who killed her?"

"She doesn't remember. She was drinking pretty hard that night. Remember health class? I think she might have blacked out."

Charlie rubs his forehead, then looks at me again. "When your grandpa told me you had issues, is this what he meant?"

"I'm not mentally ill, Charlie."

He sighs. "Isn't that what a mentally ill person would say? You wanted or needed to talk to Tori. So in your mind you were able to."

"I'll prove it to you." I know I'm taking a risk, but I'm already in over my head. "Do you have a computer I can borrow to use the internet?"

He doesn't move. "Can't you just use your phone?"

"The police took it."

With a sigh, he retrieves a laptop from the dining room table.

"When I was talking to Detective Geiger, I saw a woman in the interview room. She pushed her way through the floor and started talking to me." I click on the browser window. "She told me her name was Lisa McMasters and that her skull has been in the police evidence room for forty years. She was begging me to help her."

Charlie doesn't say anything. He just watches me with a worried expression.

I type in "Lisa McMasters" and then "missing" in the search bar. This is definitely a high-wire act, because I don't know what I'll find.

When I hit return, a few things pop up, but they're for different women who are also named Lisa McMasters. A Lisa McMasters in Hawaii posted about loving pumpkin spice lattes. Next I try "Lisa McMasters" and "prostitute," with the same lack of real results. Her name plus "truck stop," gets me several hits on Pinterest for science projects. I don't even bother trying to understand why, just go back up to the search bar and try again, this time with her name plus "North Carolina."

That does get me something. A list of people who graduated high school in 1975 in a North Carolina town I've never heard of.

I point. "I'm pretty sure that's her. She said she was from North Carolina and that she was killed in 1977."

Charlie winces. "I hate to say it, Adele, but that doesn't prove anything."

There must be some way I can shake his certainty. I try a different tack and type in the name of the man she said killed her.

"John O'Reilly" does get a hit. Pages of them, actually. The first one is a *Wikipedia* entry.

John "Johnny" O'Reilly (born August 30, 1953) is a serial killer who has been on death row at the Oregon State Penitentiary since 1983. He was convicted in the murders of three women and is the primary suspect in four more. All of O'Reilly's victims were prostitutes.

Inside me, something loosens. Like I've been holding my breath since I found Tori's body and only just now let it go.

Charlie leans in. "Who is that?"

"It's the guy she said killed her. And he's been in prison since way before we were born. There's no way I already knew about him. The only reason I do is because Lisa said she was one of his victims."

"Hmm." Charlie's brows draw together. "And what did she say happened?"

"She said he was her customer. And that he killed her and dumped her body in the woods. Later hunters found her skull but not the rest of her body. She's been in the evidence room ever since. She was begging me to tell Detective Geiger. She wants her family to know what happened to her, and she wants to be buried back in North Carolina."

"Okay, I believe—" Charlie starts.

Relief surges through me. "Oh thank God, you—"

"Let me finish. I believe that *you* believe what you're saying. But I'm afraid I don't believe it myself.

Your brain is probably just connecting little snippets of things you've read or heard and making a story out of them."

I want to scream in frustration. Charlie doesn't believe in things he can't measure, can't observe.

But is there a way he could?

"There's a cat," I say. "Or really more of a kitten. It hangs out by the dumpsters in the back of the complex."

His features pinch together. "Why are you talking about a cat, Adele? Maybe I should take you back to your grandpa."

"I'm talking about it because I'm the only one who can see it. It's dead."

"So?" He shrugs. "If you're the only one who can see it, it's not like you can show it to me."

"But all the dead are connected to their skulls by this thing that looks like a rope of mist. And if I dug in the spot where the rope disappears and found a dead cat, it would prove what I'm saying. It would prove that I'm not making things up!"

The closest thing Charlie has to a shovel or trowel is a large metal serving spoon. Five minutes later, we're standing by the dumpsters. I'm glad it's dark now, so that we're less likely to attract attention. In a low voice, I call the kitten. Finally, I see it peeping through the bushes. I put my hand down, rub my fingers together, and it skitters up to me with a questioning meow. I stroke its knobby back, feel its rib cage vibrate under my fingers. And then I trace the tether from the back of its head to the ground.

Charlie watches, his expression a strange amalgam of interest and doubt, as I take the serving spoon and dig it into the ground.

And ten minutes later, we are both looking at a jumble of what seem like gray-white sticks.

Bones.

SHARP ENOUGH TO BITE

But even the bones didn't persuade Charlie. He pointed out I've lived in my apartment complex for years. That I could have seen someone burying the kitten—or it could even have belonged to me. With every word, I felt more and more alone.

In the end, I reburied the bones and gave him back his spoon.

I've spent this morning holed up in my room, thinking about suspects and trying to avoid my grandpa and his sad eyes. I figure that Charlie's right about Ethan and Jazzmin. It's unlikely that they did it. That leaves the best suspects as Tori's dad, her creepy neighbor Mr. Conner, and our student teacher, Mr. Hardy.

The same suspects I told Detective Geiger about. But it felt like he was focused on me. In order to persuade the police to look at them more closely, I need more than just my suspicions. I need proof.

I walk out into the living room, where Grandpa is watching a football game. "I'm going to run a couple of errands." His only answer is a worried twist of the lips. But he doesn't forbid it.

I ride my bike to a Barbur Boulevard strip mall. I've seen the I-Spy Shoppe from the bus, but I've never been inside. It's sandwiched between a Thai restaurant and a tanning salon. A bell tinkles above my head when I push open the door. From behind the cash register, a clerk in his fifties with a military-short haircut glances up, then goes back to reading a magazine. The store is a single room with blank cream-colored walls and industrial-gray carpeting. It feels oddly impermanent, like tomorrow it might turn into a tattoo place or an Iranian deli.

The display case next to the door holds a variety of items designed to conceal valuables. A fake rock. A false-bottomed planter. A completely unconvincing rubber dog poop that looks more like a gag gift. There are safes made from hollowed-out books, car batteries, and a giant can of Fritos. Everything is slightly off. Like, a *can* of Fritos? They seem designed more to appeal to a nine-year-old boy than to deter thieves.

But as I move to the back of the store, the contents of the cases become sleeker and more expensive. Car bomb detectors, night-vision goggles, GPS trackers, and a brief-case that promises to greet any unauthorized user with ten thousand volts.

And one case holds a dozen recording devices disguised as something more innocuous. They look like USB drives, teddy bears, electrical outlets, and smoke detectors.

Seeing my interest, the clerk puts down his magazine and comes over. "Can I show you anything?"

"I want to be able to record conversations without the other person knowing. And I won't know where we'll be talking, so something you need to attach to a wall or anything like that won't work."

"You need to be aware that in Oregon, it's legal to record someone over the telephone without telling them. But that's not true of in-person conversations." His words sound rote.

I hesitate. But all I need is to give Detective Geiger a reason to look at the real killer. Not to prove it in court. "That's okay."

"I'd recommend one of these, then." He unlocks the back of the case and takes out five pens. Some record audio and video, some only audio. I end up choosing the cheapest. Voice activated, it can record up to eight hours of conversation. And it actually can be used as a pen. Outside the store, I take it out of its packaging. I clip it to the front strap of my backpack, then triple-check to make sure it won't come loose.

Back on my bike again, I set off for Tori's neighborhood.

But once I'm there, I'm not exactly sure what to do after I lock my bike to a speed limit sign. Things that seemed like good ideas in my bedroom or even in I-Spy now seem impossible. I'm not a spy. I'm a seventeen-year-old girl. But what choice do I have?

Taking a deep breath, I walk up to Mr. Conner's door. And then I knock.

When he answers the door, he's wearing a blue-and-red-plaid cowboy shirt that snaps up the front, topped with one of his ever-present bolo ties. This one has a silver clasp that looks like a howling wolf. Mentally, I measure the thickness of the black cord against the line I remember seeing on Tori's neck. It seems about the same.

"Hey, I don't know if you remember me," I say. "My name is Adele. I used to be friends with Tori when we were little? And I was at her party? That Saturday?" Without meaning to, I raise my intonation at the end of every sentence, like I'm an uncertain girl asking questions, not a serious adult making statements.

He nods. "Yes?"

"Remember how you offered me a ride home that night?"

"Did I?" he says mildly. When I don't say anything more, he says, "I was just concerned about you. Frankly, you seemed to be under the influence."

"Did you see Tori leave?"

"No." He shakes his head, his expression still vague and pleasant.

"Did you follow her? Because she told me that you liked to watch her."

After a long pause, he says, "Look, Adele. You seem like a nice girl. Lonely, but I understand what it's like to be lonely. What it's like to be an outcast. What it's like to feel that you are always on the outside and you can never, ever get in." As he speaks, his expression begins to morph. His faint smile becomes a grimace, showing worn ivory teeth that still look sharp enough to bite. "But you're no Nancy Drew. You're just a silly girl with an overactive imagination." He leans closer, his sour breath washing over me. "And you need to be careful, Adele. Very careful that it doesn't get the better of you."

And then he closes the door. But he doesn't slam it. He shuts it very gently, his eyes never leaving my face.

I'm shaking as I walk back out toward the street.

"Adele?" a voice says. "What are you doing here?"

It's Mrs. Rasmussen, about to get into her silver Tesla. She is still dressed in black, although the funeral was yesterday. Her face is not particularly friendly.

"I was just talking to Mr. Conner."

"Why?"

"I was wondering if he had talked to Tori that night."

After a long pause, a laugh spurts out of her. "Oh my God. Are you feeling guilty? Is that it? Just stay the hell out of this, Adele. Leave the sleuthing to the police. I can't believe you dared to show your face around here. Of course, you're the same girl who came to my Tori's funeral yesterday crying crocodile tears. Since then, I've learned the truth. The last thing you did before she died was to throw yourself at her boyfriend. You're nothing but a Judas."

Judas kissed Jesus to identify him to the soldiers. That

was a different kind of kiss, but I guess it was just as much a betrayal.

"I'm sorry, Mrs. Rasmussen. I made a mistake. I told Tori I was sorry for it, and I was. I just want to make sure the police are looking in the right places. And Tori told me Mr. Conner used to watch her when she sunbathed."

"What?" This at least seems to get through to Mrs. Rasmussen. She looks over her shoulder at his house.

I'm pretty sure whatever relationship I had with Tori's mom is irretrievably broken, so I just spill the rest of it. "Tori also told me that your husband had pushed her when he was angry at her. Even held her down. And I know he was mad when he came home early and discovered the party."

"Frank?" she says. I hear the hesitation in her voice, but then she steels herself. "Get out of here. Now. Or I'm calling the police and telling them you're stalking us. I don't ever want to see you again."

MONDAY, DECEMBER 3, 7:55 A.M.

FIGHT

Without my laptop, I have no way to listen to the recordings I made with the spy pen. Today at lunch I'll use one of the computers in the school library to review them. My conversation with Mr. Conner chilled me. It's clear there's something wrong with him—but wrong enough that he would kill a girl?

I also can't forget the venom in Mrs. Rasmussen's voice. Or the hesitation when she said her husband's name.

But so far I don't have anything to prove—or disprove—that either of them did it.

My plan is to talk to Mr. Hardy before classes start. What if Tori called him the night of the party? Earlier she had been crying in her bedroom, feeling unloved, saying she couldn't tell the truth about things. What if after kicking me out and breaking up with Luke, after the dirty dancing and the shots, she decided to demand love and/or truth from Thomas Hardy?

For him, Tori was a ticking time bomb. If she had ever told the truth about their relationship, he would have been at risk of losing everything.

The minute I get on the bus, I know things are going to be bad. Even though I'm careful to stay close to the bus driver and the adult commuters, behind me I hear Aspen muttering my name. When the bus pulls up at school and I start down the stairs, someone shoves me from behind. I stumble forward, but when I finally right myself and turn around, all I see are unsmiling faces. It could have been Aspen or any one of a half dozen people. Even Marnie bares her teeth at me. I turn and hurry away.

School doesn't start for another twenty minutes. As I walk down the hall toward Mr. Hardy's room, people turn to watch me. I'm just thankful no one says anything.

Checking to make sure the pen is still clipped to the front of my backpack, I step inside Mr. Hardy's classroom and close the door behind me. I'm in luck. We're alone. But should I need them, there are a hundred witnesses just a few feet away.

He pastes a smile on his tired face. "Oh, hello, Adele. Did you need help with something?"

I jump in with both feet. "I think maybe you're the one who needs help."

The smile disappears. "What are you talking about?"

"Why weren't you at Tori's visitation or funeral?"

His mouth opens, but there's a pause before he finds

words. Meanwhile, his fingers slide up and down the narrow fabric strap of his lanyard. "Of course, the death of any student is a tragedy, but I'm afraid I already had plans."

I want to keep him off-balance. "And you didn't think it was important to change your plans? Even though you and Tori were so . . . close?"

He shuts his eyes as if he's just heard some bad news. But when he opens them again, any trace of friendliness is gone. "What are you saying, Adele?"

"Tori told me about you. About you two." Waiting for him to fill in the blank, I wish I had pressed Tori for specifics.

He takes a step closer, close enough that if he leaned forward he could kiss me. Instead he says in a low voice, "Tori was my student. Nothing more. And if I were you, I would be very careful about spreading rumors. You, of all people, should know how dangerous they are." He reaches around me and opens the door. "Now get out."

Not knowing what else to do, I leave. I don't know any more than I did before. I think Mr. Hardy could have done it. But *did* he?

"Hey, Adele, can I ask you something?" Jazzmin says before I open my locker. Ethan's right behind her, his hand on the small of her back. They must have made up.

"Uh, sure."

"Why'd the police take you away Saturday?"

"They just wanted to talk to me some more," I say. "Because I was at the party."

Looking over her shoulder, she raises her eyebrows

at Ethan before turning back to me. "We were all at the party. But you're the only person they wanted to interview again after the funeral."

A crowd is starting to form around us. And it's getting bigger by the second.

Petra pushes through until she's standing right in front of me. "You've been jealous of Tori for years. You may have been friends back when you were little, but as she got older, she got smarter and realized she didn't need you. And you couldn't stand that she left you behind."

"*Could* Adele have done it?" a girl says behind me. It sounds like Brianna Clark.

"She's certainly big enough." I recognize Dylan's voice. "She's gotta be twice as big as Tori."

"Come on, you guys, stop it!" Charlie shouts from the edge of the crowd. "Leave her alone!" No one pays any attention. Instead of trying to get closer to help me, Charlie turns and leaves, pushing in between people.

"Did you see her at Tori's funeral?" Aspen asks the crowd. "She was smiling. Smiling!" She turns to me. "We all know what must have happened the night of the party. You tried to take Luke away from Tori, and then when she called you out on it, you killed her." Spittle flecks my face when she speaks.

"No, I didn't." My voice shakes. "I left. That's it. I left, and I went straight home."

Laquanda is at the edge of the crowd, her hand over her mouth.

"You killed her," Aspen repeats. "Everyone knows it.

The police know it. That's why they took you in for questioning."

"Just stop." My voice breaks. "Please stop."

Petra gets even closer. "Why didn't you just kill yourself instead? Instead of killing my best friend! And then you acted all sad at the viewing, but the next day you were laughing."

She gives me a two-handed push on the shoulders. I stagger back until I crash into the bank of lockers. Then I hear Luke yelling, "No! You guys. No!" And suddenly he's in front of me, putting his body between me and the two girls and the eager crowd behind them. "Come on," Luke appeals. "Leave her alone."

It doesn't work. Petra throws something at me. A pencil. It bounces off my head and lands on the floor.

"I can't believe you'd cheat on Tori with *her*!" Murphy yells.

His face a mask, Luke swings at Murphy, but Murphy ducks out of the way, and the punch grazes the side of Justin's head. With a grunt, Justin throws a punch at Luke, but Luke twists so that Justin's fist lands harmlessly on his shoulder. Then Luke hits him square in the nose. Justin staggers back, blood slicking his upper lip.

Aspen grabs my wrist and yanks. Her other hand is raised to slap me.

I swear and push her away. Her foot lands on the pencil and keeps moving. Suddenly Aspen's falling. And then she's screaming. Sitting on the floor and cradling her left arm, which bends twice, once at her elbow and then a smaller bend between her elbow and her wrist. It's clearly broken.

She looks up at me. "What did you do? Oh my God, Adele, what did you just do?"

A whistle cuts through the noise. I look up to see Ms. Chaudry pull her fingers from between her lips. Charlie is standing beside her.

She manages to project her voice above the babble. "This will stop right now, or you will all be suspended. You must disperse immediately."

In front of her, Officer Werdling is wading through the crowd. His flashlight is in his hand, and he's using it like a baton. He's coming straight toward us. Me and Luke.

Twenty minutes later, the two of us are sitting in front of Chaudry's desk. Werdling is standing behind her, his arms crossed. The nurse checked us out and pronounced us okay, with the exception of some welts and scratches. Now she's in her office putting a temporary splint on Aspen's arm before she gets taken to the hospital to be checked out.

"I am shocked at your behavior, Adele." Chaudry shakes her head. "You've never caused any problems before."

That's an understatement. If I were still taking the pills, a potato would be more likely to cause problems.

"What was this fight about?"

"Tori and I argued the night she was killed." I'm not going to mention the kissing. "People have decided that makes me a suspect."

"Yeah," Werdling says. "The police got a warrant yesterday to search your locker."

I stiffen. His words shouldn't be a surprise, but they are.

The principal folds her hands. "Tensions are running very high at Wilson right now. A lot of it is targeted at you, rightly or wrongly."

"Rightly or wrongly! I didn't kill Tori."

"I didn't say you did." Chaudry presses her fingertips together. "I only meant there's talk that Tori found the two of you in a compromising position on Saturday. People are angry on her behalf." She looks from Luke to me and then back at Luke again. Her brows draw together. I can tell she's trying to figure it out. The two of us don't go together. We're like characters from two different movies. His is a musical, all bright colors, and mine is something dour and Swedish, shot in black-and-white.

"This school has a zero-tolerance policy for violence," she continues. "That policy requires mandatory suspensions in cases like this."

"But I didn't start it," I protest. "Everyone was yelling at me and calling me names, and then they began throwing things at me and pushing me."

"Yelling is words. Nothing more. As for the pushing, I didn't say you were the only ones who will be disciplined. We will be interviewing other students."

Werdling breaks in. "I definitely saw the two of *you* fighting." He points at Luke. "It looks like you broke Justin's nose!" His finger moves to me. "And you broke Aspen's arm."

"I didn't break her arm! She grabbed me. And then she slipped on a pencil someone threw at me. That's not my fault."

Hidden by the desk, Luke puts his hand on my knee for a second. I go still, and then realize he meant me to. Shooting me a sidelong glance, he presses his lips together, signaling I should shut up. Then he releases my knee.

I realize he's not arguing back. And that I'm probably not doing myself any favors.

"That may be true, but both of your actions have had an adverse impact on our school community," Chaudry says. "You kept other students from learning, you used profane language, and you fought."

We both sit in silence. I try my best to look sorry.

"Adele, you have no disciplinary record, unlike Luke."

I glance at him, but he keeps his eyes on the principal, his face betraying nothing.

"Luke, we all understand that Tori was your girl-friend and that your emotions are understandably heightened. Given that, I am going to make a one-time exception to the suspension protocol for causing bodily injury." She takes a deep breath. "Luke, you are suspended for three days. For you, Adele, it will be five."

ALL MY SECRETS

Tears spring to my eyes. I blink them away, hoping neither Chaudry nor Werdling notices. Not tears of self-pity, but of anger. I didn't start the fight, but I'm the one being punished. And Luke is in trouble just for trying to help me.

"What about homework?" I ask. "How am I supposed to keep up with my assignments?"

"We'll email them to you," Chaudry says. "Right now, Officer Werdling will escort you to your lockers to collect your books and belongings, and then off campus. We've notified your mother, Luke, and your grandfather, Adele, but neither of them can leave work. They both want you to go straight home."

To my relief, class is still in session when we leave the office. When I open my locker, everything's been rifled through. It's a fresh reminder that I'm the main suspect. Will I ever be back here? Or will I end up in juvie or jail?

At Luke's locker, a picture of Tori is taped on the inside of the door. She wears a low-cut turquoise blouse that sets off her coloring and her cleavage. A pink piece of paper in the shape of a cartoon speech bubble next to her mouth says, "Love ya so much!!!"

Luke doesn't appear to even glance at it as he shoves books into his backpack, but the photo is all I can look at. When Tori posed for it, she had no idea she would soon be dead. The loss of her suddenly seems obscene.

"All right," Werdling says. "I'll escort you two as far as the sidewalk. Remember that neither of you is allowed to set foot on campus until your suspension is up."

"I drove here, and my car's in the parking lot," Luke says. "So I actually need to go there."

Before Werdling speaks, he adjusts his duty belt—with his gun on one side and Taser on the other—as if to remind us that he's the one who's calling the shots. "We'll walk Adele out first and then go back for your car."

Luke looks at me. "What about if I give you a ride home, Adele?"

Werdling glowers. It's clear he doesn't like the idea. But once we're off school property, he can't tell us what to do.

"I'd appreciate that." I'm barely holding it together. The idea of getting on the bus or walking the more than two miles home is almost too much.

Luke's car is a maroon Outback. The passenger seat is littered with Burgerville wrappers, parking receipts, a charging cord, and a couple of empty Starbucks cups. "Sorry about the mess," Luke says, shoveling it into the back seat, where it joins his backpack.

"It's okay." I slide into the seat and put my backpack on my lap.

We drive past Werdling, who watches us with his hands on his hips.

"You're lucky you still have your car," I say. "They took my grandpa's truck to look for evidence. I guess they're thinking I could have used it to move Tori's body."

"That old puppy nose truck? I've seen him drop you off in it. It's a classic." Luke sighs. "The police have talked to me twice, but they must figure it's not worth taking my car. I mean, Tori's in here all the time. Finding her DNA or fingerprints or whatever wouldn't tell them anything."

"The police can't even tell my grandpa when he's going to get it back. Now he's going to have to take the bus to work, and that takes nearly an hour longer each way. Plus, my grandpa loves that truck." Without warning, I burst into tears.

Hastily, Luke pulls over. "Adele, are you okay?"

"Everyone thinks I did it. The police. People at school. They all think I killed her." I drop my head into my hands.

He pats my shoulder awkwardly. "Actually, I'm pretty sure the police think *I* did it."

I lift my face. "You? Why?"

He bites his lip. "Who kills girls and women?" He answers his own question. "Boyfriends, husbands.

Ex-boyfriends and ex-husbands. Not other girls. I'm a much better suspect than you are. And they keep asking me exactly where I went after Tori made me leave. The truth is I just drove around. But that sounds bad. Like I'm lying." He offers me a sad smile. "Maybe I should have lied."

I take a deep breath. "I'm sorry I've never apologized to you." I look out the window because I can't meet his eyes.

"For what?"

"For, um, kissing you in Tori's closet?" My face burns.

"It's okay. Don't think about it."

I'm desperate to explain how what happened wasn't really my fault. "Have you taken health class yet?"

"No. Next term."

"I guess you can black out when you drink too much, too fast. Like I did at the party."

"You were really putting them back," he agrees. I shoot a glance at him, and he gives me a wry smile.

"And I never drink. Which is why I did something so stupid." I make myself say the worst of it. "My memory of the rest of that night is kind of spotty."

"You didn't seem like yourself that night." Luke swallows. "Do you remember telling everyone that really dirty joke?"

"What? No."

"Or putting your hand up under my T-shirt when we were in the closet?"

"I did?" I can't read his expression.

"I was like—whoa, Adele." He doesn't sound unhappy.

I turn away and knock my forehead into the cold window. "Oh God." I close my eyes. "Do you think I could have done it? That I could have killed her?"

"Of course not. But things don't look good for either of us." He sighs. "Look. How about if we go someplace and talk? Maybe together we could figure out what really happened to Tori. Because right now, I don't trust the police to find the truth."

Relief floods through me. "Okay."

"What about that little park across the street from the Hillsdale library? There's usually never anyone there."

When he gets out of the car, Luke brings his backpack with him, so I bring mine. The park, with just a picnic table, a slide, some swings, and a few bare trees, is deserted. Across the street, a half dozen people are gathered in front of the library, waiting for it to open.

Luke takes a seat on one side of the picnic table, and I sit on the other. Even though I'm wearing my coat, I'm cold. Luke has slipped on gloves. I wish I had some.

"You're the one who knew Tori best," I say. "Was there something going on in her life that could have led someone to kill her?"

"Tori? She had a lot of friends, and she also had a lot of enemies." He pauses a moment. "That never bothered her, not as long as everyone was paying attention. But it's hard to see anyone hating her enough to kill her."

"Who do you think did it, then? What about Mr. Conner, that creepy neighbor?"

"He's, like, ninety." He shakes his head. "Tori could beat *him* up."

"Supposedly it doesn't take that much strength to strangle someone with a rope or whatever. What if he jerked that bolo tie over her head and surprised her?" Luke still doesn't look convinced, so I move on. "Or what about her dad? I heard he came home early and was really mad when he found the party."

He tilts his head to keep his hair out of his eyes. "Yeah, but he's still her dad."

I think of Charlie and his talk about Occam's razor, of the simplest answer being true. "But her dad still fits into that whole 'suspect the boyfriend/husband' dynamic you were talking about. He's a man with a close personal relationship with her."

He shakes his head. "I just can't see it being her own father."

I move on. "And what about Mr. Hardy?"

"The teacher?" His eyebrows rise. "What about Mr. Hardy?"

Luke either doesn't know or he's faking it. If I tell him the truth, how can I make him believe me? "I heard a rumor they might have been dating. Or whatever you want to call it."

"No," he says, then repeats it with more strength. "No. Even Tori wouldn't be stupid enough to do that."

I decide to skip telling him about my pen recorder. It will just make me look weird, and besides, not one of them said anything damning. "But if we don't think of another suspect, the cops are going to keep looking at us." With my index finger, I trace the initials carved into the table. HA + PR.

"Maybe all we have to figure out is why they think that—and then work to negate it." He reaches for his backpack. "Let's each make a list of reasons the police might think we did it. Then we can trade lists and figure out how to counteract those things."

He takes out a notebook and a pen, and I do the same. When I'm done, my list looks like this:

1. *Tori used to be my friend but then decided she wasn't.*
2. *She told people I was mentally ill.*
3. *She made fun of me for being different and for being overweight.*
4. *She embarrassed me in front of everyone at the party.*
5. *I don't remember everything about that night.*

"Done?" Luke asks. When I nod, we trade notebooks. His list reads:

The cops always look at the boyfriend first.

And things had been over between Tori and me for a long time. We weren't making each other happy anymore.

Every time I'd try to break up, Tori would flirt with other guys just to make me jealous, to force us back together.

Lots of people have heard us argue.

And I have no alibi.

Luke raises his head from reading my paper. "Oh, that part about embarrassing you at the party goes for me, too. Give me my notebook back for a second."

"Let's trade. Because I have the alibi problem, too."

We both add to our lists and then swap them again.

He looks back down at mine. "What's this about being mentally ill? Is that like how Tori told me you sometimes saw things? Do the police know that?"

"They know that a long time ago I was diagnosed with schizophrenia. But now I'm sure that the diagnosis is wrong."

"But the police don't know that." He pushes my notebook back to me. "You should add that to the list."

I do, right after not having an alibi.

7. *I have been diagnosed as schizophrenic.*

I pass the notebook back. He gives me a half smile. Now Luke knows all my secrets. But he doesn't care.

WOULD IT SURPRISE
YOU TO KNOW

Across the street, the library doors open, and people begin to file in. "Do you mind if I take a break and head over there?" I ask Luke. "I have to go to the bathroom."

"No worries." He smiles. "I'm not going anyplace."

I walk through the double doors feeling lighter than I have since I found Tori's body. At least Luke believes I'm innocent.

But the lightness doesn't last. Because that's not enough, is it? The problem with both our lists is that everything on them is true. And none of it looks good. Not for me. Not for Luke.

When I push open the door to go back outside, I spot a plain dark blue sedan parked behind Luke's Subaru. Charlie's uncle, the detective, is walking up to the picnic table, straight toward Luke. My stomach does a flip.

I want to run, but I make myself walk unhurriedly back across the street. I try to act unconcerned, but I can't even remember how I normally hold my head or swing my arms.

"Adele," the detective says. He has the same high cheekbones as Charlie, and his eyes are the same shade of golden brown. "I don't think we've been formally introduced. I'm Detective Lauderdale. Detective Geiger and I are working Tori Rasmussen's case together."

Mechanically, I shake his outstretched hand.

He answers my unspoken question about how he knew where to find us. "I went by the school to talk to Luke. When I learned he wasn't there, I called him, and he told me where you were. And actually we wanted to speak to both of you. Luke's already agreed to come down to the station. We just have a few more questions."

Luke and I exchange a glance.

"Okay," I say slowly. There doesn't seem to be any other choice. I remind myself that all the evidence against us is circumstantial. Maybe things don't look good, but they'll never turn up anything proving one of us did it.

Lauderdale insists we take his car. Luke sits up front with him, while I sit in the back. Everyone's mostly quiet. Luke's face is open and relaxed. I take deep breaths from the abdomen and tell myself we'll be fine.

When we get off the elevator, Detective Geiger is waiting in the hall. "Hello, Adele," he says. "I'm glad you were able to come by. I just have a few more questions for you."

"Okay." I turn to Luke, but Lauderdale is already ushering him into an interview room. I realize we aren't going to be questioned together, and my courage starts to desert me.

Everything is the same as before. The same interview room, the same chairs, the same gray file folder, the same tape recorder, the same verbal reminder that I am free to leave at any time. I brace myself, waiting for Lisa's head to push through the floor again.

But it doesn't.

"This thing is snowballing, Adele." With cupped hands, Geiger pulls one knee toward his chest and leans back. "There are going to be arrests, and soon. But if you tell us everything you know, you'll be in a better position with the grand jury."

A better position? "But I've already told you everything." I'm still distracted, looking at the floor behind him. Lisa told me she mostly just slept. Maybe she's still sleeping.

"We've been working this case hard. We've been talking to everybody: Jazzmin and Ethan, Petra and Laquanda, Justin and Murphy, Dylan and Sofia. We know what happened that Saturday. And now it's time for you to do the right thing and clear up the inconsistencies. You're hiding something, Adele."

"But I'm not." At least not anything I can tell him.

Geiger groans in disgust and turns away. After a long stretch of silence, he turns back, his face set. "We know you're a good person in a bad situation. Help us to see your side, Adele. Help us to understand what happened that night."

"Nothing happened. I just left the party and went home."

He continues as if I hadn't spoken. "Did you just snap? It's understandable, really. Everyone says she was awful to you that night. That she publicly humiliated you. Did you feel like you had to finally shut her up?"

"What? No!"

Geiger won't stop. "That girl had a temper. Everyone says so. Did she catch up with you and threaten you? Were you afraid for your life? Were you forced to do something first before she did something to you?"

"I didn't touch her, I swear." I remember the feeling of her weeping in my arms, but what I just said is true, at least if you're talking about the living Tori.

Geiger's chair is on wheels, and he keeps inching it closer. He offers me another excuse, another out. "Sometimes it might feel like you're just standing on the outside, watching what happens. Like it's not really you doing it at all. Is that what it was like Saturday night?"

"I didn't do it," I say between gritted teeth.

He leans back and crosses his arms, shaking his head in disappointment. "Do you know what Measure 11 is, Adele?"

"It's some kind of law about kids being tried as adults."

"Right. Under Oregon law, even if you're as young as fifteen, if you commit certain types of crimes, you must be tried as an adult and you must go to prison for a legally mandated period." Geiger's voice punches each *must*. "Those crimes include murder. And the mandated term for murder is twenty-five years."

It only takes a second to add it up. I would be forty-two when I got out. I close my eyes and swallow.

"Would it surprise you to know that two people claim to have seen you arguing with Tori in the parking lot of your apartment building that night?"

Startled, I open my eyes. "What? Who?"

He doesn't answer, just asks another question. "Would it surprise you to know that another witness saw a girl—described as 'a bigger girl'—getting out of an old truck in the back parking lot of Gabriel Park around midnight Saturday? And that she appeared to be dragging something heavy into the woods?"

I try to imagine myself dragging Tori. But her dress wasn't dirty, and neither were her feet. Although does that really mean anything if she was already dead when she was dragged? After all, the Tori I see doesn't show any marks from the autopsy. She looks exactly the way she did at the moment of her death.

"I swear to you, the last time I saw Tori alive was when I left the party. And then I went home. There are other people you need to be looking at." I offer him the same suspects I did before. Only it's even more important that he believe me. "What about that creepy neighbor of hers, Mr. Conner, the one I told you wanted to give me a ride? Or how about her dad? I heard he came home early, and he got mad about the party. And there's our student teacher, Mr. Hardy—I think there was something going on between him and Tori."

Geiger is silent for a long time, mulling over what I just said. Finally, he's listening to me.

And then he speaks, and I realize I can't read him at all. "Adele, stop throwing dirt in my eyes. You're flailing around, trying to get me to look at anyone but you." He makes a disgusted sound. "We know you practically grew up at the Rasmussens'. And how do you repay them? By casting aspersions on Mr. Rasmussen. And by denying Tori's family the peace of having an answer."

There's a knock on the door and then it opens. Detective Lauderdale sticks his head inside. "Mark, would you mind stepping out for a second?"

I feel like I've been spinning around in an industrial-sized dryer. I don't know what to think about all the things Geiger just said. I miss Lisa's commentary. I put my hand over my mouth. "Lisa?" I whisper.

But the floor stays flat, and my head isn't aching. Like Rebecca at the museum, Lisa said my presence woke her up. So why isn't she here now?

Geiger comes back in. He slaps his palms together, like he's dusting them off, like he's just finished something. "Detective Lauderdale tells me that Luke has already been very forthcoming. You need to get ahead of this thing, Adele, or his story is the only one that's going to be told. And in Luke's story, you don't look too good."

All the blood leaves my face. "Why? What did he say?" How does this fit with what Luke said in the park?

How can he have turned against me? It feels like I'm falling. I put my hand out and steady myself against the wall.

"Was it the two of you that night, working together? Was it all Luke's idea?"

"No! Stop it! I didn't even see him after I left the party."

"Only one person can cut a deal, Adele. And if I were you, I'd want to be that person. Otherwise, this could all get hung around your neck."

Lisa said it was legal for the police to lie to suspects. I grab hold of that thought. Maybe Geiger's just making everything up. Maybe no one saw me in the apartment parking lot or at the park. Maybe Luke isn't telling them anything.

Maybe.

Geiger's blue eyes drill into me. He won't be satisfied until I say I did it. It would be so easy to embrace his version of me, his version of what happened. If I took the blame, then his incessant questions would finally stop.

But I can't. I won't. I press my lips together and say nothing.

He sighs. "Adele, do you know what we found in your grandpa's truck?" It's clear he thinks I know the answer. But I don't. And I don't think I want to.

"No." Can he hear the tremble in my voice?

He reaches into a folder and then passes me two photos. One shows a dozen strands of red hair stuck against gray fabric. I realize it's the back of the truck's passenger seat. On the floor next to it is a yellow ruler. The second photo is taken at an angle. Hidden underneath the seat is a high-heeled slip-on sandal.

It's Tori's.

MONDAY, DECEMBER 3, 4:17 P.M.

THE LAST PIECE
OF THE PUZZLE

After Detective Geiger tells me he is going to take me back home, I ask, "What about Luke?"

He shrugs as he pulls his car keys from his pocket. "Let's not worry about him, Adele. You need to be thinking about yourself now."

When Geiger pulls into our parking lot, I get out of the car without saying goodbye. I head for the stairs, my head bowed under the rain that has begun to fall. Lunchtime has come and gone, but I'm not hungry at all. Once inside the apartment, I walk straight to my bedroom. I kick off my shoes, fall on my bed, and pull the covers over my head.

Sleep is the only escape I can think of. It always worked when I was on my meds. Only now it won't come. And when I finally manage to doze off, Tori haunts my dreams, crying again in my arms. Lisa McMasters makes an appearance, too. Both of them demand I help them.

I awake tangled in the sheets. I'm sure Detective Geiger was lying when he claimed that in Luke's version of what happened that Saturday night, I didn't look so good.

Pretty sure, anyway.

But does it really matter what Luke said? Because the hair and the shoe can't be explained away. Geiger said they were testing them for DNA.

I think we both know the DNA will be Tori's.

The only explanation is that I got drunk, blacked out, and killed Tori.

I figure the detective is just waiting for that last piece of the puzzle to snap into place before he goes to the grand jury and presents the case for why I should be arrested for Tori's murder. It's not like he needs to worry about me going on the lam. Where would I go? I'm seventeen. I've got no money and no passport, and now I don't even have access to a vehicle.

A knock at the front door makes me start. Have they come for me already?

But when I look through the peephole, it's Charlie standing on the front step, nervously shifting from foot to foot.

I open the door.

"I came by to apologize for this morning. For going to get Officer Werdling. I thought he could stop those people from attacking you." He sighs. His eyes never leave my face. "I never thought you'd be the one to get in trouble."

Stepping back, I let him in. "Getting suspended from school is the least of my troubles." I slump down on Grandpa's recliner.

"What do you mean?" He sits on the couch.

"You know your uncle, the detective? I got a chance to meet him today."

"What?" Charlie looks surprised, then worried. "Where?"

"When he took me and Luke down to the station." My eyes sting as the reality of my situation hits me again.

"You were with Luke?" Charlie tilts his head like that's the important part.

"We both got suspended for fighting. We ended up at that little park by the library, talking about why we were suspects. Luke thought things looked bad for him because he was Tori's boyfriend."

"He's not wrong," Charlie says. "If a girl or woman is murdered, more than half the time it's by her current or ex-partner."

"Maybe he doesn't look good, but I look worse. Because your uncle came looking for us and drove us downtown. He took Luke into one interview room, and I ended up back with Detective Geiger. And Geiger showed me these pictures of what they found when they searched my grandpa's truck. Behind the seat, there was this clump of red hair and a shoe." I blink, and a tear rolls down my face. "Charlie, it was one of Tori's sandals. I remember them from the party."

He covers his face with his hands.

"And it's true I had access to my grandpa's truck that night. And that my memory is spotty. I drank a lot that night, and I never drink. I must have gotten black-out drunk. Luke said I was telling dirty jokes at the party and doing other stuff I would never normally do." I'm not going to detail the bit about my hand under Luke's shirt. "Maybe I'll never remember. But I'm starting to think the police are right. I must have done it."

Taking his hands from his face, Charlie pats the air as if comforting me from a distance. "Okay, I'll admit it doesn't look good, but there's got to be an alternative explanation."

"I was trying to figure out who could have done it. I even went to that I-Spy Shoppe and bought this pen that makes secret recordings. I tried to confront Mr. Conner and Mr. Hardy. I even talked to Mrs. Rasmussen about her husband. But nobody admitted anything. They were mostly just mad at me."

"Adele!" Charlie winces. "You were taking a huge risk doing that. You could have ended up just as dead as Tori."

"It didn't really matter." My laugh is bitter. "I should have just held the pen and interviewed myself."

Charlie's inner geek gets the better of him. "Do you have it? What's it look like?"

I get my backpack from the floor, unclip the pen, and hand it to him. "You can actually write with it. It's voice activated, so I guess it's even recording this." I unscrew it and show him the USB inside. "You just plug that into a computer, and you can download it or listen to the recording."

"Can I listen to it?"

"Sure, I guess." I put it in his long-fingered hand. "Only what's the point? With Tori's shoe and hair in my grandpa's truck, the answer to who did it is pretty clear." I poke myself in the chest. "Me. Even if I don't remember." My voice breaks on the last word.

Charlie hesitates, and then says rapidly, "Now, don't get mad, but is there any chance it could have been your *grandfather*?"

"What? No!" Except for a second, I find myself remembering the angry way Grandpa talked about Tori. But it doesn't add up. "He thinks *I* did it. He keeps looking at me with tears in his eyes and shaking his head. He wouldn't do that if he was really the one who did it." And then I think of the clincher. "Besides, haven't you noticed his hands? He's got arthritis. They hardly work at all. I doubt he could even hold on to the rope or whatever it was that killed her."

Charlie doesn't look completely convinced. "Have you noticed any bruises on the edges of his fingers? Or anyone else's fingers?"

"No," I say slowly. "Why?"

"I've been doing some reading." He takes his headphones out of his pocket. After raising one knee, he loops the cord around it, then wraps the ends once around each hand to tighten it. He pulls back hard. After he releases the cord, he holds out his hands to show me the lines it left on his pinky fingers. "It's pretty common when the ligature is narrow for it to leave bruises on the outside edges of the killer's fingers."

I hold out my untouched hands, fingers spread, and turn them back and forth. "Maybe it wouldn't leave any marks if you were wearing gloves. Which I wasn't, but I doubt they'd believe that."

"But I believe you, Adele." His eyes are steady on my own. "Maybe it's not logical, but I do. I may not believe you can talk to the dead, but I don't think you killed Tori."

I sigh. "I didn't even see Lisa when I was talking to Geiger today. Maybe I *am* all messed up, Charlie. I mean, parts of Saturday night are a blur." I look away from his warm gaze. "I must have really done it. Occam's razor and all that."

ALL MY NERVE ENDINGS

Twenty minutes after Charlie leaves, there's another knock on the door. I figure he's come back. But when I open it, Luke is standing on our welcome mat. His gloved hands hold a bouquet of pink and white roses wrapped in green florist's paper. At the sight of it, a flood of warmth runs from my scalp to my toes.

Then he opens his mouth, and I realize what an idiot I am.

"Hey, I'm on my way to visit Tori's grave, but I thought I'd stop by first and see how things went with the cops today. When I left, they told me you were already gone."

I let him inside. "Everything was okay up until the point Geiger showed me photos of what they found in the back of my grandpa's truck. A sandal and some red hair."

"The truck?" Luke stills. "But you rode your bike to the party."

"Yeah, but my grandpa's friends picked him up that night to go bowling. I guess it's possible that I came back and got the truck. That's what the police seem to think happened. And that sandal in the photo sure looked like the ones Tori was wearing that night."

He presses his lips together. "There has to be another explanation, Adele. Maybe someone planted them."

"The simplest explanation is that I did it. It's the only thing that makes sense. I got drunk, blacked out, and then killed her."

He shakes his head. "Did you tell the cops that?"

"No. Not yet. I don't want it to be true, but I think it has to be."

Luke closes his eyes and takes a deep breath. Then he opens them again. "I don't believe it," he says decisively. "Besides, if they really think it was you, then why did they keep badgering *me*? They even told me you were saying I'd done it."

"What? I never said that." Relief washes over me. "They were lying to both of us. They told me *you* were telling stories about *me*."

Luke stabs the air with his index finger. "If they lied about that, maybe they were the ones who put that hair and shoe in your grandpa's truck!"

"It might be legal for them to lie. But it's a big step from that to planting evidence." And Lisa said Geiger was a good cop, but it's hard to figure out how to work that into conversation. Assuming there even is a Lisa.

"So it's okay for the cops to tell a lie to trick people into telling the truth? That's still messed up." Luke pushes back the hair that's fallen over his eyes. "You and me, we've got to stick together. If we do that, then they'll have to figure out who really killed Tori."

I nod, grateful that Luke believes in me. Right now, even I don't believe in me.

He clears his throat. "The other reason I stopped by is that I have a favor to ask."

"What?"

He looks down. "Will you go to Tori's grave with me?"

I take a half step back. "I don't think I can."

"Please." His voice cracks. "Please, Adele, I can't do it alone."

"My grandpa will be worried if I'm not here when he comes home." Then I remember about his truck. "Although I guess that won't be for at least another hour, now that he has to take the bus."

"We won't be gone long." Luke raises the bouquet. "I just want to put these on Tori's grave. I've been thinking about her all day. I mean, sure, things were rough between us, but she didn't deserve what happened."

In the end, it's not so much his plea that decides me but the thought of Tori seeing him and the flowers. It will mean so much to her to know that Luke still loves her.

"Okay. Let me get my coat." I also loop a scarf around my neck to camouflage any whispers to Tori.

Outside, it's still raining. "Sorry," Luke says, "I parked across the street. I didn't know if there'd be any spaces in your lot."

Once we get in, Luke hands me the flowers to hold.

I sniff, but they must be greenhouse grown, because they don't smell of anything.

The cemetery is just a couple of miles away. I've never been inside the grounds. Before I started taking medicine, I used to see an old man emerge from a grave near the fence whenever we drove by. Dressed in a hospital gown, his cheeks sunken, his eyes drilling into me until I closed my own.

I sense more than see the old man as we pull into the lot. Pain stabs my temple, but I tell myself I can do anything for a few minutes.

There's a chain across the road that leads into the cemetery and a sign saying it's open only until sunset. The sun has just slipped under the horizon. There's still some light, but it's fading rapidly.

"I guess we can't go in," I tell Luke.

"It will only take a few minutes." He gracefully steps over the chain, but I have to steady myself by putting my hand on his shoulder to cross.

We head up the hill. My eyes are adjusting to the fading light, but even so I have to be careful. The cemetery is old, so rather than just metal plaques lying flat against neatly trimmed grass, there are elaborate granite and marble tombstones and statues, as well as trees, ponds, and fountains.

And for me, there are the dead. All around, people begin to push their way out of the earth. Some eagerly, some so slowly I can tell they don't want to be awakened. An old man in a plaid shirt and worn jeans, his face mottled and gray. A gaunt young woman in pink pajamas, her dirty-blond hair hanging in strings around her face. A nine- or ten-year-old kid so broken he shouldn't be able to stand, yet he does.

All of them have their eyes fastened on my face.

Most are as solid as the living. A few have wavering edges. An old man who walks out of a marble tomb the size of a small garden shed is nearly translucent. Some of the dead stretch and yawn, scratch themselves absently. Some stare at me, looking confused.

And they all begin to talk.

"Is someone here?"

"Is it the rapture?"

"Who woke me?"

"It's that girl," the old man by the fence calls. "She can see us."

The thing is, I can see less and less. Not just because it's dusk, but because of the pain in my head. If it felt like an ice pick with Tori and Lisa, now it's a stainless steel spear.

"Come on, Adele," Luke says over his shoulder as he starts to walk on the grass. "Her grave's just up here."

He ducks under the nearly bare branch of a maple tree, and there it is. A raw brown rectangle of dirt. There's no stone yet, but a bouquet of white flowers is stuck into the ground at the head.

And then Tori climbs out of all that dirt without disturbing a single grain. There's not a smudge on her perfect alabaster arms and shoulders. Even the rain just bounces off her. It's like she's been sprayed with water-proofing. She practically glows.

"Luke! And Adele?" She looks from me to him and back again. "Why are you here with him?"

I whisper through the scarf over my mouth. "He didn't want to come alone."

Stepping forward, she strokes Luke's face. "Baby, can't you hear me? I miss you so much." Her voice breaks.

Oblivious to her, Luke kneels at the top of her grave and begins to unwind the green paper from around his bouquet. Tori stands over him and rests her hands on his shoulders. A container set flush against the ground already holds a bouquet. He's trying to stick his in with it, but there isn't room for both.

On all sides, more dead are appearing. A woman holding a toddler on her hip. A man in a three-piece suit. A family of five, all of them except the mother with hawk-like noses.

Luke has pulled out the other bouquet and laid it on the ground. Now he replaces it with his own.

"Oh, Luke." Tori drops to her knees in front of him. She's ugly crying now, or it would be ugly crying if her body could still make tears.

Getting to his feet, he swipes at his knees. For a minute he and Tori overlap.

"Oh, Adele, don't cry," he says, reaching out to me. My right eye is leaking from the pain.

"Even if I didn't do it, it's still my fault. I set everything in motion. If I hadn't kissed you . . ."

He pulls me close to him, his mouth against my ear. "What happened that night—it made me realize I was done with her. Maybe I messed up, but it was only once.

Tori wanted me to forgive her for all the things she's done." He snorts angrily. "When she sits on other guys' laps and kisses them. Right in front of me. Or dirty dances with them. And then the next day she always cries—cried—and said she was sorry and that she didn't remember. Which is such a lie."

"What?" Tori says angrily.

I pull back so my words aren't muffled by his shoulder. "It's possible she really *doesn't* remember. She has—had—blackouts. From drinking."

She's standing behind him now, her hands fisted on her hips.

"So? Does that excuse her? She still did those things. It's not like someone put a gun to her head." He gives me a crooked smile. "Just like I knew what I was doing when I kissed you. I've always liked you, Adele. But because I was an idiot, I didn't want to say anything. I was still trying to be loyal to Tori. But that night, when I realized who I was hiding with, I couldn't stop myself. I just had to kiss you. And damn the consequences."

Wait. Luke kissed *me*?

Tori stamps her foot. "You jerk! I'm not even cold in my grave, and you're trying to hit on my friend."

While she's talking, I run back through the last few years. The way Luke's eyes never quite focus on me. Has he just been protecting himself, not admitting his feelings?

"Tori and I, we were on our last legs, but I denied it. Denied how I felt about you. But I can't deny it anymore." He bends his head until his lips touch mine.

"Wait. What? No, it's too soon," I whisper, putting my hands on his chest but not really pushing him away. I close my eyes so I don't see Tori or any of the other dead. I ignore the pain in my head.

"No, it's not. This is the only life we have, and we don't know when it will end. What if we're like Tori, dead tomorrow?"

Luke's lips are so soft, but then they press into me hard. I freeze. My heart pulses in my ears. My skin feels tight. It's like I'm dwindling, like there isn't enough air.

"I can't believe you two!" Tori says.

I can't believe this is happening. I've spent years watching Luke. This is what I wanted, right? Luke finally lifts his mouth from mine, his lips trailing kisses around my throat. He gathers my hair, pushes down my scarf, and starts to kiss the back of my neck.

He moves behind me. Now the only things connecting us are his lips on my nape. It's like all my nerve endings are concentrated there. Tori keeps protesting, but I can't pay any attention.

And then suddenly something scrapes down my face and viciously yanks me backward.

NOWHERE TO GO

Luke is doing his best to strangle me, yanking back on the cord or rope or whatever it is that's now around my neck.

"It was you!" Tori screams. "You're the one who killed me!"

Swearing, she begins to pummel him, but the pressure around my throat doesn't ease. It's clear Luke feels nothing. Hears nothing. But when one of her blows misses him, pain explodes in my jaw.

"You're just like Tori," Luke hisses in my ear. "Don't know when to be quiet."

With my left hand, I manage to grab what I realize is a leather dog leash on the far side of Luke's gloved hand. I try to pull it away from my neck, but Luke is stronger than me. The layers of my scarf offer a scant cushion, and the leash is over my trachea, not my carotid arteries. From what I read online researching Tori's death, these two things mean I will have a little more time than she did.

Not that that's going to make any difference in the end.

"Stop it, Luke!" Tori screams. "Don't!" Around us, other spirits are beginning to comment and call out, encouraging me to fight.

"We were making up that night but then she told me about Mr. Hardy. About how he was a real man, not a boy. She wouldn't stop talking. I just needed her to shut up."

"It didn't mean anything!" Tori's voice breaks.

I twist and turn and tuck my chin, desperately trying to find an angle that will still allow oxygen to get to my brain. I kick backward, but my foot just glances off his shins.

He shifts his grip, and the leash tightens even further, making me cough. "I can't go to prison. I'm going to college. The cops are already looking at you. When they find your body hanging over Tori's grave with that list you wrote in your pocket, it'll all make sense."

My vision starts to dwindle like water swirling down a drain.

"Shh, Adele, shh," Luke whispers, his breath warm on my ear. "Don't struggle. You'll only make it worse."

It would be so easy to give up. To stop. To get it over with. I feel my body start to go limp.

"Adele!" Tori screams in my face. "Don't let him do this!" And then she slaps me.

The shock of it wakes me up. My eyes fly open. I arch back, pushing the top of my head hard under Luke's chin. The pressure eases infinitesimally, allowing me to turn my left shoulder into him. I remember Justin at Tori's party, demonstrating how to fight.

Drawing back my right hand, I make a fist. Then I punch Luke in the throat as hard as I can.

A grunt is forced from his mouth. The leash loosens as he bends double. He braces his hands on his knees, coughing and gagging.

"Run, Adele!" Tori shouts. "Run!

I throw the leash to one side as I start to run. My eyes have adjusted to the dark, but where should I go? I could try to make it back to the deserted parking lot, but that's where Luke will expect me to go.

I risk a glance behind me. He's still bent over, but it's not like I knocked him out. Pretty soon he'll be after me.

"Help her, you guys!" Tori yells. She's stretched to the end of her tether. "Tell Adele where to hide. Tell her where to go. Save her from the guy who killed me!"

I've spent years denying that the spirits of the dead existed. Now I need their help.

The woman with a toddler on her hip points up the hill. "Go that way."

My feet slipping on the wet grass, I tear up the rise, zigzagging my way through the spirits. I push between a middle-aged couple and then leap over their tombstone, which is shaped like an open book.

When Luke starts chasing me, he'll have it easy. He just has to avoid the tombstones. I have to avoid the dead.

A woman dressed in blue, bald and far too thin, points to the right. "If you keep going that way, I think there's a road."

I charge off in that direction. But almost hidden in the grass, a baby lies on its back, gurgling. I switch course in midstride to avoid stepping on it—and instead end up tripping over its tombstone that's topped with a lamb.

Wham! I land hard, knocking the air out of me.

"He's coming," a man's voice behind me calls. "Hurry!"

I scramble to my feet, hoping the soft rain falling around us will cover my gasping breaths. But Luke's a legend on the football field. I'll never be able to put enough distance between us.

Frantically, I look for something I could use to defend myself. There's a metal trash can, only it's chained to a pipe. Next to a tree sits a stack of orange cones and a half dozen plastic gallon jugs filled with water. None of it looks useful.

Hoping the spirits hear me as well as Tori does, I whisper an appeal. "Is there any kind of weapon I can use?"

"There's a flag stuck on my grave," a man's voice calls off to my right.

I change course and run toward the man dressed in fatigues. There's a black hole in the middle of his forehead. Leaning down, I grab the flag from his grave. As I run, I use my index finger to test the point that was stuck in the ground. It's sharp, but it's not like it's a knife. It's just a wooden stake. I imagine trying to stab Luke with it. Too bad he's not a vampire. It would probably only truly hurt him if I stabbed him in the eye. And even if my aim in a fight could be that good, I'm not sure I'm capable of it.

"There's an open grave over here," calls a middle-aged woman dressed in just her underwear. Her body is pockmarked with stab wounds. "Maybe you could hide in it."

But when I reach it, it's just a narrow, open rectangle about five feet deep. Each of the four sides is draped with a strip of Astroturf that falls a few feet into the grave. Next to it is a pile of dirt covered with a green tarp. Three boards are laid widthwise across the grave, either to hold down the Astroturf or to warn people away or both. I think about jumping in. I could crouch down and pray Luke runs past.

But if he finds me, there will be nowhere to go.

Instead I kick two of the boards out of the way and pick up the third. Then I dart behind a double gravestone that's taller than me. "Tell me when he's coming," I whisper to the elderly couple buried there.

"He's about twenty feet away," the old woman says a half minute later.

But even tucked behind their tombstone, I can see the cone of light from Luke's phone pushing ahead of him, hear his hoarse, panting breaths. He stops at the foot of the new grave and peers down.

Which is when I jump out behind him, holding the board like a bat. I swing it as hard as I can.

It hits his head with a sound like a cantaloupe falling to the floor. Luke takes a step forward into the empty air. He tumbles into the grave.

And then down the hill, I hear someone yelling, "Adele? Adele? Where are you?"

It's Charlie. His voice sounds close. At the entrance to the cemetery are red and blue flashing lights.

"Watch out!" the lady in her underwear screams.

Just as a hand closes around my ankle.

SATURDAY, DECEMBER 22, 11:58 A.M.

ENERGY IS NEVER LOST

It's amazing how much can change in three weeks, I think as
I clump up the cemetery hill on my crutches. This is
the first time I've been here since the night Luke tried to
kill me. This time Charlie's at my side. And Tori now
has a white marble headstone.

She's sitting with her back against it, legs crossed at
the ankles. Charlie and I are bundled up against the
December chill, but Tori's comfortable in her halter dress.
We wave at each other and exchange smiles. "Hey, Tori."

Charlie looks from me to the grave and back again.
He's agreed to visit, but I think it's still a struggle for him
to believe.

"You look good, Tori," I say. "If you have to be stuck
in one outfit forever, that's not a bad one." I turn to
Charlie, who's spreading out the tan plaid blanket he

carried up here. "It's this halter dress that's an amazing shade of blue-green. Like a peacock feather."

"Die young and leave a beautiful corpse. Isn't that what they always say?" Tori shrugs one shoulder. "Only now I realize how caught up in appearances I was. Like with Luke. I overlooked a lot of things he did just because he was so beautiful."

"You're not the only one who was guilty of thinking Luke's beautiful outside must have reflected his inside," I say as Charlie takes my crutches.

"Yeah, but I was pretty shallow in general. Like I stopped being friends with you because I was worried what people might think about me. But even though I pretended not to care, you know what? I still have—I mean had—that SpongeBob SquarePants squirt gun you gave me on my sixth birthday. That was your favorite thing ever. And you gave it to me without hesitation."

"Because you were my best friend." Rather than repeating everything Tori says to Charlie, I've decided to stick to the important stuff. I figure he can pick up the rest from listening to my half of the conversation.

After taking my crutches, he helps me lower myself to the blanket. Luke broke my ankle when he tried to yank me down into the empty grave with him. When the cops and Charlie showed up, I was dangling half in and half out of the hole, kicking Luke with my unbroken leg.

At school, I've gone from pariah to hero. I'm not comfortable with either role. But I've started hanging out with Laquanda. It turns out she makes all that jewelry she wears, and she's been showing me how. I also signed up to take an Italian cooking class over winter break. I don't know exactly where my life is going, just that it's opening up.

Charlie's part of that. Later that night, he insisted on riding with me in the ambulance. We've talked every day since. About Luke. What we were like as kids. My mom. His mom, who left when he was just a baby. What we want to do after we graduate. And about what I can see and why that might be.

Now the other dead eavesdrop as Charlie and I catch Tori up on what happened after the police came.

"Okay," I say to Tori, "Luke told the police that after you kicked him out of the party, he sat in his car in front of your house, trying to decide whether to break up with you for good. And then you came out and tapped on his window. You guys ended up in Gabriel Park, making out in his car. But then you told him about Mr. Hardy, and he snapped. He strangled you with the charging cord that was plugged into his lighter. Later he noticed he had bruises on his fingers from wrapping the cord around them, so he pounded the wall at school to cover them up with more bruises. And when he realized that I was becoming the main suspect, he planted your sandal and some of your hair in my grandpa's truck."

Charlie takes up the story. "They didn't find any of your fingerprints, Tori, in the truck itself. But they did find smudges on the passenger side window that looked like they were made by gloves. And they recovered a pair of gloves from a storm drain near the apartment. When they turned them inside out, they found Luke's prints. They think he used a coat hanger to open the door lock and then planted the hair and shoe."

I chime in. "The thing is, Tori, I can see how he had your shoes, but that clump of hair? When did he take that?"

Tori leans forward. "What about when he bent down and hugged my body at the viewing? I was crying so hard when he did that, but I remember seeing my head kind of jerk. He must have been yanking out some hair. He was already thinking about framing someone."

I relay what she said to Charlie, then echo her next words: "'Tori is asking how you knew to come to the cemetery to rescue me."

"Adele had bought this recorder that looks like a pen. It's voice activated, and she'd been questioning people she thought were suspects, but without really learning anything. I asked if I could listen to it. Not only did I hear her talk to your neighbor and your mom and Mr. Hardy, I also heard this big fight at school that ended with Adele and Luke getting suspended. And afterward, Luke told Adele that they should each make a list of why the police might think they were guilty. That recording ended when Adele said she had to go to the bathroom." His eyes cut to me and then back in Tori's direction. "I was about to unplug the pen's USB when I heard this scrabbling sound. It was Luke searching through Adele's backpack, looking for her list. I heard him rip it out, and then he muttered something under his breath like, 'Wait till the cops read this. Once you're taken care of, Tori's murder's going to be an open-and-shut case.'

"I went to warn Adele, but she was already getting into Luke's car across the street. The cops had taken her cell phone, so I couldn't call her. I jumped on my bike and followed Luke's car. I kept thinking I'd lose them, but with rush hour traffic, I was able to keep them in sight. I was also trying to call my uncle, who's a detective, but it's not that easy if you're riding your bike in the rain in heavy traffic."

Tori looks from Charlie to me and back again. "Adele can see me, but you'll never be able to. What made you believe her?"

After I repeat her question, Charlie says, "To be honest, I didn't. Not at first. I thought she had mental problems. But that didn't change the fact that Luke was trying to frame her."

He explains about how Lisa McMasters made him change his mind. After I told Charlie about her forty-year-old murder, he'd decided to take a chance and send his uncle an anonymous email about Lisa. He included links to John O'Reilly's *Wikipedia* page and the list of graduates from a North Carolina high school.

That email was the reason I hadn't been able to see Lisa during my second police interview. Her skull had already been taken away for more tests. A few days after Luke's arrest, his uncle mentioned to Charlie that an anonymous tip had ended up solving a forty-year-old case.

"He thinks whoever sent it must be someone who

knew what happened back in the day but was afraid to come forward." Charlie sighs. "But when I heard the outcome, I had to ask myself how you knew all these details about a death that happened before we were born. It's like solving a crime. When the evidence and facts lead you away from your working theory, you have to be willing to see things in a new light. So what you had said about being able to see the dead had to be real."

Charlie and I have discussed what would happen if people found out about my ability. The living would surely demand that I interrogate the dead—find out who killed them, or where the money went, or even just ask for assurances or advice from their loved ones. Historians would want me to corroborate details. Scientists would want to study me.

And some of those people might not want to give me any choice in the matter.

I'm going to have to figure out how to navigate the world without ever giving away my abilities.

Some people are born with perfect pitch or are able to multiply two five-digit numbers in their heads. Charlie thinks that what I have is a genetic twist on schizophrenia. And that it must be dominant, since my mom and grandma had it.

But what about people with real schizophrenia? The drugs that work for them are the ones that stopped me from seeing the dead, so are schizophrenics also telling some kind of truth?

Like so much else, I just don't know.

Sitting on the blanket, squinting in the bright winter

sunshine, I suddenly realize that I don't have a headache, even though I'm surrounded by the dead. But for once I'm no longer fighting the idea that they are there.

I risk asking the question that's been bothering me. "So, Tori, are you disappointed that you're still here, even though Luke's been caught?"

She shrugs. "Now that I know what happened, it's gotten a lot easier. It feels like the world's fading away, or maybe I am. I sleep most of the time, or whatever you want to call it. In fact, you being here is the only reason I'm awake right now. I know I kept asking you to visit me, but I think I'd rather just stay asleep and wait to see what comes next. I don't think I'll be here forever."

"What do you mean?" I ask.

Tori waves a hand to indicate the other spirits. "Have you noticed that some of us are see-through? And people who've been here a long time say that folks from really old graves keep getting fainter and fainter. A couple have just disappeared. And people who're cremated—they say you never see them at all, even if the cremains are buried here on the grounds."

Charlie looks thoughtful as I catch him up on what Tori said. "In physics, the law of conservation of energy says that energy is never lost. It's just transformed. And the skull holds the brain, which runs on electrical impulses. Maybe even after death some energy is left behind. Something so small that only certain people can perceive it if the skull still exists. That's only a hypothesis, but it fits the evidence."

"So then what happens when those spirits completely disappear?" Tori asks. While I repeat the question, the dead around us lean forward, all awaiting Charlie's answer.

"I don't know," he says simply. "I guess it still comes down to the same question humans have always asked: What's next?"

Tori bites her lip. "What do you think will be next for Luke?" She looks down, feigning disinterest, but as I repeat her words to Charlie, I can tell she still cares.

"The law says that he has to be tried as an adult and that the minimum term for murder is twenty-five years. My uncle thinks that's probably all he'll get. He presents well, he's young, and his parents can afford to buy the best defense attorney. Plus, your death wasn't premeditated, even though the attack on Adele was."

I half expect Tori to protest, to say that her life is worth more than twenty-five years, but she doesn't. Instead she says, "What about you two?"

"What do you mean?" I ask Adele as Charlie gives me a questioning look.

"It's obvious that you like each other. What's next for you?"

Charlie is watching me expectantly, waiting for me to repeat Tori's words. I look at his intelligent brown eyes, his sharp cheekbones, his lips that I suddenly remember are soft and warm.

"Something good, I think. Something very good."

Charlie turns to me. "What are you guys talking about?"

"Just a little girl talk," I say with a smile. And then Tori gives me a wink.

———

The parking lot is empty except for Charlie's dad's old sports car. Charlie opens the passenger door and tosses the folded blanket on the tiny rear seat. With a couple of awkward hops, I turn my back to the open door and put one hand on the roof and the other on the doorframe so he can take my crutches.

As Charlie leans in to maneuver them past my seat and into the back, his shoulder brushes my stomach. I can feel the heat from his body even through our coats. When he straightens up, his face is just a few inches from mine. I suck in a breath. Slowly, as if afraid he'll startle me, he puts his cool palms on either side of my face. For a long moment we just look at each other.

Partly to steady myself and partly to lose myself, I put my arms around him. Then I close my eyes and press my mouth to Charlie's. Just as I remember, his lips are soft and warm, and he tastes like peppermint.

If the dead are watching, I don't care. This is about us, and we're alive.

ACKNOWLEDGMENTS

Therapist Helen Paris told me how she would approach an adolescent who thought they could talk to the dead. Caron Pruiett, a forensic scientist who providentially sat next to me on a plane a few years ago, answered my question about ligatures. And former cop and current author Robin Burcell advised me in many ways large and small.

I'd also like to thank staff at the Multnomah County Library, who helped me obtain copies of many Oregon Trail diaries. Author Cat Winters offered advice about using historically accurate language. And Lizzy Knobel of the End of the Oregon Trail Interpretive & Visitor Information Center patiently answered some strange questions.

My editor, Christy Ottaviano, helped make this book the best it could be. I can always count on Jessica Anderson to be unflaggingly cheerful as she keeps everything organized. April Ward designed the beautiful cover. At various times, Morgan Rath, Molly Brouillette, and Amanda Mustafic coordinated events across a dozen states. Other wonderful folks at Henry Holt include Jennifer Healey, Lucy Del Priore, Katie Halata, Kathryn Little, and Allison Verost.